JOHN MACKAY returns to his Hebridean roots for his third novel, which, like *The Road Dance* and *Heartland*, is set in Lewis. John is the anchorman on Scottish TV's evening news programme *Scotland Today* and has reported on many of the major news stories in Scotland in recent times. He is married with two sons and lives in Renfrewshire.

By the same author:

The Road Dance, Luath Press, 2002
Heartland, Luath Press, 2004

Last of the Line

JOHN MacKAY

Luath Press Limited

EDINBURGH

www.luath.co.uk

First published 2006
Reprinted 2007

ISBN (10): 1-905222-55-6
ISBN (13): 978-1-9-0522255-1

The paper used in this book is recyclable.
It is made from low chlorine pulps produced in a low
energy, low emission manner from renewable forests.

Printed and bound by Bell & Bain Ltd., Glasgow
Typeset in 11 point Sabon

Acknowledgements

Runrig for giving us a voice.
Mairi Maciver and my brother Donald for their knowledge.
Joan MacKinnon of South Uist.
Margaret Ann Laing and Rosemary MacLennan for their support.
Donald Slessor.
Magda, Sheila and the Edinburgh MacKays.
Welcome to Emma Harvie.
And J, S and R always.

For Ally
'...the blood is strong...'

I

THE CALL CAME from a place far away where the dark was deep and the only sound was the fading breath of a woman on the edge of eternity.

'Mr MacCarl. It's time.'

Outside, the lights of the night spread and faded through the room, the party people laughed and squealed on the streets and an isolated horn blared.

'She asked for you.'

'I'm sorry?'

'Mary. She asked to see you.'

'She wants to see me? Now? Who is this? Can I speak to her?'

The woman's voice on the other end lost none of its soft lilt, but it delivered a harsh message.

'If she makes this night of it she won't see the next.'

'What? What happened? Has she been in an accident?'

'No. She has been ill, seriously ill. The end is near.'

'Oh Christ! I had no idea.'

There was no response.

'I'll see what I can do.'

'She really wants to see you.'

'Yeah, okay.' He sighed, muttering thanks as an afterthought.

Cal MacCarl swung his legs out of the bed, the stripped wood of the floor was cold under his feet. It took a moment for the time on the bedside alarm to register.

'Who was that?' the girl beside him asked, her long blonde hair covering her face, her voice muffled by the pillow.

'My aunt. She's dying.'

'She phoned to tell you? Can't be that serious,' mumbled Lisa dismissively.

'It wasn't her who phoned,' Cal snapped, defensive yet at the same time uncomfortable about the sharpness of his reaction.

'Mmmm. Come back to bed,' she murmured, already falling back to sleep.

Cal sat with his head in his hands and inhaled deeply. This had come without warning. How could he not have known? He realised guiltily he couldn't even remember when they had last spoken. Mary would have known. She'd have remembered.

A decision had to be made. The temptation was there to slip back under the duvet and fold himself around Lisa's warm curves. She would welcome him warmly in the morning and then he could get a plane. But he wouldn't sleep now, he knew he wouldn't. His mind was so alert, he could actually feel the blood coursing through his system and his nerves prickling. If he drove through the night, he might catch the early ferry. Besides, it would be good to have the car with him on the island.

He would be cutting it fine, but the roads would be clear this early and he should make it. He padded through to the bathroom and stepped under the power shower. The blast of cold water instantly invigorated him. Goose bumps pimpled across his body.

He dried himself with a towel grabbed from the floor. The bathroom was a mess. Party clothes lay strewn where they had been thrown, tired soap suds floated flatly in the sunken bath and there were steam stains on the wall mirrors. The two empty champagne glasses made him think, but it hadn't been that much. He would risk it.

Within five minutes he was dressed in clothes grabbed from the walk-in wardrobe. A Ted Baker shirt, Armani jeans and Hogan shoes. He put a change of clothes and a pair of Rockport boots into a holdall, crushing his Berghaus jacket in beside them. Cal's toiletries bag was always packed and ready in the bathroom. He gave himself a cursory glance in the mirror and was unhappy with his hair, but time was against him and he assured himself that where he was going, no one would care.

The girl in his bed slept throughout all this activity. Was it wrong to leave her without so much as a goodbye? Would she even care? Did he?

Cal turned his back on her and left the flat. The lift slid smoothly open almost immediately. Probably no one had used it since he and Lisa had returned whenever it was before. A button from his shirt lay on the floor. The passion had kicked in quickly. He picked it up and put it in his pocket.

The man looking back from the lift mirror made an effort to look younger than his mid thirties. He was of average height and build, his body trim from the gym and his dark hair still thick enough to be styled. His flat, even tan suggested sun beds rather than sunshine. His clothes were never more than six months old.

The lift dropped quickly through the five floors to the garage. Cal's Audi sports car was his joy. He had paid way too much for it, but he needed the image. The big deal would come soon and he would be free from the barely sustainable debt that funded his lifestyle. He was never less than sure of that. There was nothing like getting out on the road with the roof down, bass beat thumping, leaving others in his slipstream. And when did you ever see guys in these cars alone?

It was too cold to have the roof down yet. As soon as the electronic security door rolled open to expose the street, he was away. A taxi blasted its horn at him as he screeched out in front of it. He roared on scornfully. Taxi drivers had no room to complain about anyone else's driving.

The traffic lights frustrated him as he raced from one red to the next, but soon he was on the main highway, relishing the surge of the turbo power. It took twenty minutes to leave the sodium lights of the city behind.

As he drove along the side of Loch Lomond, the moonlight playing on its waters, his thoughts returned to Aunt Mary, always the same, so warm, seemingly ageless. But death had summoned her now. Too early, and he knew that she would accept the call.

Mary MacCarl was part of a different life, a separate world almost. She came from a time when his parents were alive and the family ties remained strong. She still knew him as Calum.

He had left all that behind, but, gentle though she was, his aunt had a resilient streak. The monthly calls always came, even if he didn't always respond to the stilted messages she sometimes left on his answer machine. Always a card for his birthday and a gift at Christmas. Guilt caught him occasionally when he realised he'd neglected to return one of her calls. It was just that he had so much going on and the old connections slowed things down. If she resented it, she never gave any sign.

Cal was all she had. He was the son of her older brother and she was his only blood. 'We're all that's left,' she had said, lightly enough, 'and when I'm gone, you'll be the last of the line.'

Was it her subtle way of pressuring him into settling down? Cal was sensitive to the slightest suggestion of disapproval. He'd tried to make a success of his life and no one had the right to pass judgement on the way he lived it, yet he was always touchy that they might. He had his father to curse for that.

'If you're trying to marry me off, forget it,' he cautioned her once, disguising it as a tease. 'It wasn't good enough for you. Why should it be for me?'

He couldn't remember what she had said, but he did recall a flicker of hurt. He had never broached the subject again.

The southern section of the road was wide and sweeping and Cal relished the freedom of it, pushing the speedometer beyond a hundred miles an hour. He zipped past the few vehicles that appeared in front of him, roaring beyond them almost before they knew he was there. He was very familiar with this stretch. Barely any distance from the city, some of the best golfing, water sports and luxury living were to be found on the banks of the famous loch and Cal indulged himself regularly. It wasn't all pleasure though, it was also a good way of playing at friends with people who could be useful.

He slowed down towards the northern tip of the loch where the road narrowed, twisting round ragged rock faces, picking up speed again to surge through the great gorge of Glencoe. The craggy majesty of the mountains was lost in the darkness. Across the Ballachulish Bridge, past the beautiful setting of Onich and he was soon in the 1960s-style concrete centre of Fort William. Ben Nevis, the country's highest mountain, loomed out of the first morning light. Then, once more away, into the freedom of the country. This was driving!

North-east along the banks of the amusingly named Loch Lochy, north-west again towards Wester Ross, past the stunning Queen's View on the way to Kyle of Lochalsh and the bridge span over the sea to Skye.

The glens and mountains were never more glorious than in the birth of a new morning, though Cal saw nothing but the hypnotic road markings stretching ahead, judging the corners he could cut and the straights when the accelerator could hit the floor.

The romantic Isle of Skye was carved through in less than an hour, the grandeur of the Cuillins quickly left as shadows in his rear view mirror. He crested the final hill above Uig with ten minutes to spare. The Caledonian MacBrayne ferry, with its familiar black, white and red livery, was waiting at the pier below.

He pulled in behind the other cars lined up for boarding, got out for the first time since he'd left Glasgow and felt the stiffness in his legs as he walked over to the ticket office.

'And when will you be returning, sir?' asked the man behind the desk.

The straightforward question threw Cal. He had set out without seriously considering when he might return, just a vague idea that it would be quickly. But he didn't know what awaited him on the other side of the sea-crossing.

What would be expected of him? It was hard to think of Mary lying ill and impossible to imagine what he might be able to do for her. She couldn't be left on her own, not if her condition was as grave as he'd been told by the woman on the phone. And who had she been? A nurse, maybe. So would she leave when he arrived? And there would be a funeral. As Mary's closest kin, would he be expected to organise it? Questions flooded through his head.

'I'll just leave the return open, shall I?' suggested the clerk helpfully.

Leaving the office, Cal began to question why he was here. Was it reluctant duty? If so, then he could deny her and no one would know, no one who mattered anyway. Who could blame him? He could do nothing for her and his time would be best used dealing with the business pressures at home.

There was another motivation that made him uncomfortable, but which he couldn't deny. Aunt Mary was a woman with a low maintenance life. Cal was all she had and Cal needed money. He wanted to be sure that what was hers came to him.

Back at the car, he took in his surroundings for the first

time. The stark simplicity of sea and land, mountain and moor. The wind-burnt, craggy face of a fisherman on the pier. A housewife walking on the road with a bag of messages. Aunt Mary was one of these people, undemanding, unobtrusive and honest. All his life she'd asked nothing of him. Only now, as she lay dying, she'd made a simple request. He convinced himself that it was more than greed and duty that had sent him on this journey. His conscience would not forgive him if he failed her. After this all the ties would be gone.

2

WAITING FOR THE ferry, Cal calculated on his palmtop computer what he might expect to inherit. Mary had never been one for spending money on herself, so there might be a couple of grand in her savings and she was canny enough to have taken out insurance to pay for the funeral.

The house would be his. It might sell for about a third of what he would get for a city house of similar size. If he did it up he might get more, but he needed the money now. There would be no shortage of buyers seeking the island idyll. He could sell it off quickly.

Cal's entrepreneurial ambitions too often outstripped his means and much of his energy was taken up borrowing to pay debts. His income base was property, buying rundown flats, holding them for a couple of months and then returning them to the market. He was prepared to tart up the decor but he avoided anything structural. Usually he made a couple of thousand on each transaction.

But Cal aspired to more. The high life attracted him, and he had a point to prove, even if only to himself. His car, his apartment, his clothes, all represented the success he wanted to be, but his income could not sustain his outlays. He lacked the inside knowledge that would give him that crucial advantage as a speculator. On the two occasions he had secured more upmarket properties, there had been a temporary slump in the market and his resources had been drained dry by the time he had sold them. One had even been sold at a loss.

That was part of his dilemma over coming to see his aunt. Finally his networking had paid dividends. Lisa, who worked for an established estate agent, had given him a tip that the owner of a large Georgian townhouse had just died and her family were seeking a quick sale because they lived abroad. It would need work, but there was a fat profit to be made. Cal had been expecting to make his move over the next couple of days and he and Lisa had been celebrating their imminent pay off all last night. And now this. He didn't want to lose out by not being on the spot. On the bright side, there was the prospect of his inheritance.

The metal snake of cars started to move. He drove into the belly of the roll-on roll-off ferry and had to follow the casual directions of a shiphand waving him closer to other vehicles than he thought was really safe. There would be a chip in the black pearl paintwork, of that he was sure.

A short time later the ferry eased away from the pier in a low growl of engines and splashing of ropes. Cal was seated in the cafeteria, the large, salt-stained windows giving a view of the land sliding away. Soon the swell of the sea gently lifted and rolled the boat.

Cal walked out on deck. The fresh breeze tugged at his hair and seagulls provided a noisy accompaniment from the stern, their eyes ever alert to any edible scrap. A young girl, overseen by her father, was throwing crusts of bread overboard, laughing gleefully as two or three birds squabbled over them. One younger gull was sharp enough to catch a morsel before it hit the water. The girl pointed excitedly to her dad, who laughed indulgently.

When he was a similar age, the voyage had been an adventure for Cal. The sight of the waves frothing against isolated beaches and rocks was magical and by the journey's end it was if he'd been borne away to a different life. When had it all changed? And why? It was uncomfortable to think of it now. Rebellion mostly, he supposed. A reaction to everything his father had wanted him to be.

They oscillated at different frequencies, Cal and his father, causing constant collision and friction. At its core was Cal's rejection of his roots. His heritage was of no interest to him and his father's strong, slow accent was a source of constant embarrassment to the city boy. The annual holiday home to the islands lacked the variety of the holiday camps, coastal resorts and foreign trips his contemporaries enjoyed.

Cal had also rebelled against the strictures of the church. His parents were devoted Sabbatarians, which caused him much humiliation. 'How can ye no' play fitba' on a Sunday?' That burned deep into a boy who just wanted to fit in. 'Take pride in who you are and where you're from,' his father had admonished him. 'I do. I'm from the city.' It was a running feud.

His father had given up the crofting, fishing life to which he was born to come to the mainland and join the police, persuaded by his wife that the city would give any children they might have a better start. That's why Cal's sloth and arrogance galled him so, particularly as the boy grew older and bolder and there were no siblings to make a comparison. 'You're no son of mine,' his father had cursed more than once. His mother had kept her own counsel, trying to maintain harmony. Sometimes she would try to strengthen the bond when they were alone. 'Your father is trying to do what he thinks best for you,' she would say.

Cal remembered these conversations with regret. His mother had died an early death, when he was only eighteen. It was a miserable time. Her body had withered before them. She had been so stoical, confined to a chair and then, finally, to her bed. Whatever she knew, she never acknowledged to him that she would not survive. And when the end came, suddenly, he missed the chance to tell her how much he loved her.

His father became a brooding, impotent presence. They had rattled about the tenement flat, trying to keep out of each other's way. Mary had come down to stay with them for a while, bringing a warmth and life that helped Cal through his grief.

Mary was light and flighty, so unlike her brother, and he found fault with everything she did. The tears in her eyes when she kissed Cal goodbye were the first he'd ever seen from her. 'You be sure to come and see me,' she'd implored.

Not long after that, Cal moved into a room in a student flat and left his father to fester. Even university had been a source of tension between them. His father thought Cal should aim for medicine, law, the ministry or teaching and had been appalled when he had opted for business studies.

'Business is the way to make money,' Cal had argued.

'What's money, when you can do good?'

'I wouldn't expect you to know about money,' had been Cal's retort. And so it had gone on.

His father died before he could retire back to the island he loved, his body and mind taut with resentment at all around him.

Mary was all Cal had left and she made every effort to maintain the bond. There were cards and letters and each year she would come to see him. 'I've come to the city to find a man,' she'd joke. He made time for her and she asked for no more, but it seemed incongruous to him to spend time with his aunt. Still, her heart was so big and he enjoyed her spoiling him.

Reflecting back to his school holidays, he saw that it had been the lack of choice that he had resented. The actual holidays had been fun, especially when he travelled up on his own as soon as the schools finished. For a couple of weeks it was just him and Mary and she allowed him untrammelled freedom. Restrictions would be imposed once again when his father's leave began and his folks arrived. But it was then that he could see the man his father might have been. They would go fishing together and for a time there was peace between them.

Now he was back. It had been twenty years and more. Perhaps it was time to bury the sourness of the past. He had been away too long.

He spent almost the entire crossing of the Minch out on deck, lost in the hypnotic trance of the water, the movement of the sea never rising beyond a gentle swell. They docked at Tarbert in Harris. The port was little more than a village at a neck of land, with the Minch on one side and the mighty Atlantic on the other.

Soon the Audi was bouncing from the ramp onto the pier. To the south were some of the best unspoilt beaches in the world, miles of empty white sands. Cal's journey was taking him north.

Since his last visit, the old single track road had been widened and resurfaced. It had been a trial of a journey before, stuck behind the slow vehicles which had disembarked ahead of you. Now, Cal could zoom past two and three cars at a time. But the zig-zagging twist down the side of the Clisham mountain was a real test, and his heart jumped when he felt the rear end swing as he took one hairpin bend just too fast, yet the screech of the tyres and the wisp of smoke thrilled him at the same time. This was truly burning rubber. He imagined that with some sunshine, this could be like the roads of Monte Carlo. The dramatic beauty of Loch Seaforth cutting into the land was lost to him as he pushed northwards out of Harris and into Lewis, the fabled heather isle.

More than the roads had changed. The thatch-covered, stone-built blackhouses that had lasted a century and more, were fallen monuments to a lifestyle long gone. Even the sort of dwellings with which he'd been familiar, with their dormer windows and chimneys at the gable ends, looked cold and bare. So many houses now were large, ranch-type spreads, and he speculated that they would be beyond the pocket of most city dwellers.

The village names were different too. In his youth they had all been anglicised on the road signs, but a concerted effort to protect the indigenous Gaelic language had seen them revert back to their traditional spellings; names drawn from the Norse and the Gaelic that had so shaped the island culture. Many of these small, struggling communities had been settled longer than the self-important cities of the mainland.

Having driven north half the length of Lewis, Cal left the island's east coast and headed towards the wilder west. Buildings changed, the cars and the clothes, but the landscape remained as ever it had been. The heather moorland that smothered the land, the rocks that heaved out from the peatbog and the ocean. Timeless. And restless.

Emerging from the hinterland of the moor to the coastal townships, he knew he was almost there. In little more than an hour he had completed a journey that would have taken his grandfather more than a day.

He drove by the lochside, past the church, to the crossroads. The main road swung north-east but beyond the old stone bridge he took the branch road west. This was single-track again and he took the bends cautiously, remembering to keep left to avoid oncoming vehicles but also aware that a miscalculation would send his wheels off the verge. The road began to meander more steeply and folds of land slipped away to reveal lochs and stunning rock formations.

The house sat on a plateau at the very top of the hill which then fell away to the sea. It seemed an odd place to build a home, exposed as it was to the gales roaring in from the Atlantic. Mary could have told him why, but he'd never been interested enough to ask. This was the house in which his father had been born and raised. That was all he knew.

Cal pulled into a patch of hard packed mud and stone next to the gate, careful to avoid the drainage ditch, then switched off the engine.

The only sound was the sough of the wind round the car, seeking a gap through which to sneak. Sheep, disturbed by his arrival, returned to chomping at the grass in a neighbouring croft. A lone seagull glided in the breeze from the sea. The blend of peat smoke and brine in the air took him straight back to childhood. Yet something was out of place. In times before Aunt Mary would already have been out of the door to greet him. But not today.

3

ON THE WROUGHT-IRON gate, flakes of sky-blue paint scrapped for dominance with the brown of the rust. His father had painted it years ago. In the sea air, any metal left exposed corroded rapidly. He lifted the latch and used both hands to swing it back. Atolls of wild grass and moss strung their way up the length of the concrete path that had been the cause of another row with his old man, who had laid it with no help from Cal. Now it all just looked so old and in need of repair.

The front door faced onto the road, but he had never known it to be used. The storm doors were closed and the lock and handle were rusty. The path split in two, petering out to the left as it reached the wall of the old blackhouse. To the right, it led to a small porch at the back. This was never locked during the day and unless the weather was foul, it was rarely closed. Now it was.

He rapped on the glass panes, twisted the heavy handle and pushed it open, scraping the linoleum on the floor as he did so. It brought him straight into the kitchen. The silence was unnerving.

'Hello,' he called self-consciously.

A teapot sat on the stove. Intermittent dribbles pushed up the lid and sizzled on a hotplate heated by the fire directly below.

Cal went towards the glass-panelled door that separated the kitchen from the living room and as he did so he heard a floorboard creak and saw a shadow moving towards him. He stepped back and the door swung open. It was not his aunt. He had known from the speed of movement that it wouldn't be. He was confronted by a woman he didn't recognise, in her thirties with dark hair pulled back in a pony-tail. Her eyes were dark and warm. She wore a blue shirt over a white T-shirt, jeans and white trainers that gave her an air of athleticism.

'Hallo,' the woman said quietly. 'You must be Calum.'

This must be the woman who had phoned him in Glasgow. 'People know me as Cal,' he replied.

There was an awkward pause. Cal realised he was the stranger here.

'How is she?'

'Asleep.'

'Still with us then?' It sounded callous even to him.

'Your aunt is still breathing, yes.' The woman looked at him steadily. 'You've had a long journey. Can I get you a cup of tea?'

'I'd really prefer to see Mary.'

'She's asleep. Perhaps it would be best to leave her for now.'

'She *will* waken though? She'll know I came?'

'I hope so.'

She made her way to a cupboard and removed a bone china cup. She may be a stranger to him, but she clearly knew the house.

'I'm Mairi. From in the road.'

'Shouldn't Mary be in hospital?'

'She wanted to be in her own home. The doctors were happy

enough when I said I would stay with her. They've been very good, a nurse has been calling daily. Palliative care is all that's left, keeping the pain away.'

'I didn't even know,' sighed Cal.

'No, you wouldn't.' If it was a dig, it was subtly delivered.

She brought over a cup of tea and laid it on the kitchen table. He sat down and she offered him a selection of biscuits on one of his aunt's decorative plates. He had no appetite.

'Is there any hope?' he asked weakly.

Mairi grimaced and shook her head.

Cal sipped the tea. It was the strong, strong, scalding tea favoured by the older island folk, made with loose leaves, a big spoonful for each cup and always 'one for the pot'. It was too strong for his palate now, even the sugar left an aftertaste.

Mairi stood against the stainless steel towel rail on the stove, both hands wrapped around her cup. She waited for him to speak.

'How long have you been staying here?' he asked directly.

'For the past two nights. There was no one else who could.'

'Well, I'm grateful to you for that.'

'Mary's a wonderful woman. She's been good to me.'

Cal stared hard at the rug on the worn linoleum. Outside the wind played with the grass and somewhere a clock chimed the hour.

'Did she say why she wanted to see me?'

'Maybe there are things she has to say.' Mairi finished her tea.

'Now that you're here I'll go back home to get some things done.'

Cal looked startled.

'I'll be back. My number is on the pad by the phone if you have to call me.'

'Okay. Good. Yeah, good.'

She pulled on her anorak. Cal didn't want her to go. He didn't know her, but she was in control and would be calm and practical through whatever lay ahead. She would know what to do. In contrast, he felt an unfamiliar gnawing in his stomach. He stood up uncertainly, shoving his hands into his trouser pockets to stop from fidgeting, effectively blocking her exit, then awkwardly moved out of her way, hoping that she stay after all.

She sensed his unease. 'Listen out for her. It's unlikely she'll be needing anything. Just the fact that someone is there with her… there's nothing else you need to do. I'll see to her when I come back.'

Cal nodded and watched her walk round the corner of the house, the wind flapping her anorak.

He was shaking. Mary was approaching death and he would have to be there for her. His ability for sales showmanship would count for nothing in the room next door. He would have to rely on his basic humanity stripped bare and he was unsure whether it was up to the task.

The living room was cool compared to the kitchen. Although the heavy drapes had been pulled back, the light that penetrated the thick net curtains was absorbed by the room, the dark carpet, the wood of the furniture and the brown leather of the settee.

Cal walked into the hall and listened outside the bedroom door, delaying having to confront what lay behind it. Finally, he pushed it open. He was struck immediately by the heat of the room, a swirl of bedroom mustiness, body odour and perfume.

Daylight glowed in burnished amber through the tawny curtains. He could see Mary's shape on the bed and his breathing eased a little now that reality had usurped the fear of anticipation. She was on her back, her head resting on two pillows, her mouth slightly open and her face sunken. Her breathing was shallow and intermittent.

There was a chair next to the bed, a wicker armchair that he had never seen before. Beside it lay a women's magazine and a bag from which knitting needles protruded. The chair creaked as he sat down and the sound caused Mary to stir. There was a change in her breathing and an almost imperceptible movement of her head. Then her eyes flickered open.

Cal tensed. What could he say that wouldn't alarm her? She spoke first.

'Calum?' Her voice was weak and tired.

'Yes Aunt Mary, it's me.'

She took a deeper breath and turned her head towards him.

'Oh my dear, you came.' The words were whispered.

'Of course I came.' He felt better now, talking with her.

She breathed again. 'Maybe you could open the curtains to let in some light.'

The chair creaked again as he pulled himself out of it and moved over the draw back the curtains. The light, grey again, fell across the bed. He could see her hair irregularly fanned out on the pillow. It struck Cal that he had never before seen Mary in bed. She had always been up and about.

He sat down again. The chair was slung low, and his head was level with hers.

Her hand moved across the bedcover towards him and he rested his own gently on top of it. She tried to pull herself up, but the effort was beyond her.

'Here, I'll help you,' he said earnestly. Putting her head onto his shoulder and supporting her back with one hand, he eased her forward and pulled the pillows up against the headboard behind her. He could feel her rib cage and shoulder blades pressing through the cotton of her nightdress. How frail she was. Delicately, he laid her back on the pillows again.

She closed her eyes, concentrating on catching her breath, her chest barely moving. Cal sat still and waited.

Mary's hand stretched towards the black leather-bound Bible that had rested on her bedside table for a lifetime.

'Would you like me to read for you?' asked Cal gently.

Her chin moved closer to her chest in an almost imperceptible nod.

He thumbed through the thin, well read pages. As a child he would have known an appropriate passage, but all that inculcated knowledge had long dissipated. He scanned the flickering leaves, hoping that he might chance upon something that would touch his memory. Matthew. Mark. Luke. The Gospels. John. *John*. Why did John strike a chord? From his mother's funeral. What was it? Chapter Eleven. It all came back to him. Jesus comforting the sisters of the dead Lazarus. It seemed right. His throat was thick as he read out loud. 'I am the resurrection and the life. He who believes in me will live, even though he dies.'

Cal wished he could have read in the Gaelic, Mary's mother tongue, the way she had most often heard these words through the years. But he sensed that she found calm enough in what he said. Soon she drifted back to sleep. He sat watching her breathe for an indeterminate time before falling asleep himself, the combination of a late night and the early start overwhelming him.

When he was woken by the sound of a movement in the house, it took some moments for his mind to catch up. When it did, he jumped up and leant across Mary, fearful that she had already gone. The seconds were long before her shallow breath fell again.

Footsteps came lightly across the hall and there was a gentle tap. The floor creaked as Cal moved to the door and pulled it ajar. It was Mairi. She appeared to start a little when she saw him, her hand moving protectively to her chest. Cal couldn't stop a smile.

'How is she?'

'Just the same.'

Mairi retreated back towards the kitchen. 'Did she ask for anything?'

'No, nothing at all,' Cal replied reassuringly.

Mairi switched on a light just as he rubbed his hands vigorously over his face. She would know he had been sleeping.

'She did ask for something actually,' he added quickly, to demonstrate that he had been attentive. 'Her Bible. She wanted me to read it to her.'

Mairi nodded. 'Look, I've brought something in case you haven't eaten. It's just some chilli.' She gestured towards a small casserole dish on the kitchen table.

'Great!' Cal hadn't realised how hungry he was. 'You shouldn't have, but thanks all the same.'

He sat down and realised he had nothing to eat the food with, but Mairi was already bringing him a fork from a drawer. He smiled his thanks.

'You know this place well.'

'It's like I said, Mary was a good friend.' She corrected herself. '*Is* a good friend.'

Cal was already scooping the chilli into his mouth.

'Don't you want a plate?'

He looked at her, embarrassed.

'No, this is fine. Thanks.'

Mairi stood by the oven range again.

'Have you thought about what you're going to do? Will you be staying here?'

'I haven't thought of anything except getting here,' he said, licking his teeth.

'It's not a problem if you want to stay at the hotel. I've been here the last couple of nights.'

Cal sighed. 'The thing is, I'm here because she asked me to come. She was awake for a short spell, but I haven't really spoken to her. She's sleeping now. I don't know when she'll waken again... and she might not, I suppose. Anyway, she asked me to be here and that's what I'd better do. How are you fixed?'

'I can be here. It's not a problem.'

'How long d'you think it'll be?' Cal grimaced. 'I didn't mean it to come out like that.'

'She was failing fast last night and that's why I called you. But, she seems to have rallied a bit since I told her you were coming.'

'Do you think she might pull through?'

'The doctor said it was a matter of time.'

Cal finished the chilli and leant back in the chair. Mairi was looking at him, waiting for him to decide.

'I'll certainly be here tonight. I'm sure you could do with a break.'

Mairi chewed on her lip and it was Cal's turn to watch her. She was clearly uncertain.

'Have you got other things to do?' Cal's question was a leading one. He was intrigued by this woman.

'It's okay.'

'What about family?'

'They're old enough.'

'What about your husband?'

'He's dead.'

'I'm sorry. I didn't mean to pry,' Cal lied. 'Look, I'm going to stay. I don't want you feeling you have to.'

'I know, I know. It's just that Mary…' She paused to take a breath. 'Well, it's like I told you.'

Cal took the casserole dish over to the sink. As he got close to Mairi, she moved away from him. 'I'll just go and check on her,' she murmured. She left the kitchen and came back a few moments later. 'Still asleep.'

As Mairi pulled on her anorak, Cal took in her slender figure.

'I'll go now and give you time with her.'

'Thank you,' he said, 'for everything.'

She smiled sadly at him and the tears welled up.

'Don't be silly,' she said, sniffing. 'Mary is special. I'll miss her.' Then her tears spilled out. She pulled a paper hankie from her pocket and wiped them away. Cal felt helpless. Embracing her would be inappropriate and the words that came to him seemed insensitive. Defeated, he leaned back against the stove, his head bowed.

'I'm sorry,' she said, flustered. 'I'll be off.'

She pulled the door open.

'Mairi,' Cal said suddenly, 'I don't want you thinking I don't care. I was asleep when you called this morning and what I said didn't come out right. Please understand that Mary was special to me too. I maybe wasn't very attentive, but she was always part of my life.'

Why did he so want this woman to believe him?

Mairi stood at the door, looking at him, her eyes soft and red from her tears.

'I just wanted you to know that,' he said, gesturing openly with his hands.

'I know,' she said. 'You came didn't you?'

4

CAL SAT WITH Mary, her occasional shallow breaths the only sign of life. At one point he went for a walk through the house to keep himself awake.

The living room and bedroom were the only ones on the ground floor of the original structure, their windows flanking the unused front door. Both opened onto the lobby, which was gloomy because the outside storm doors were closed and the only light came through small, curtained side windows. A flight of stairs led up, doubling back on itself before arriving at the upper floor. A small toilet had been built beneath the stairs. Mary had joked with him that prior to that you had to go outside and hope the wind wasn't strong. There was barely any room to stand up straight in it, but it served its purpose.

There were two large bedrooms upstairs and a small area on the short landing, barely a room, that had been used for various purposes over the decades. Cal remembered sleeping there on a camp bed. Mary had evidently used it these past years to store an array of items that were beyond their best, but which she thought might come in useful again. There were a couple of chairs, an old Singer sewing machine, a stack of books ranging from faded paperbacks to hardback volumes, dating back many decades. Cal wondered what their value might be. Right at the back was the old camp bed, the springs stiff with rust.

The room above Mary's had been the one his parents slept in when they came on holiday. It had barely changed since, in all those years. There was a dark mahogany wardrobe with metal handles shaped like oyster shells, and next to it a chest of drawers with smaller versions of the same handles. A full-length swivel mirror stood by the window. At the back wall was a bed with an iron frame and a mahogany headboard. Next to it was a small cabinet that matched the wardrobe and a standard lamp with an old tasselled shade. The furniture was old but of the best quality. Even now the drawers slid open smoothly. He loved this room, with its sloping ceiling and dormer window that looked out across the road and down the croft towards the sea.

It had been many years since the other bedroom had been occupied, but it was little different from its twin along the landing. It smelt musty and he went over to open the window, which was so stiff that he only managed to raise it by a couple of inches, sending two spiders scuttling away. Air flowed in, causing the net curtain to stir.

It had been too large a house for Mary, she had said so herself often enough, but she would never have left. It wasn't just a house, it was her home, as it had been home to many others in the family down through the years. Their photographs were everywhere. Formally posed pictures, sepia tinted with faded gilt frames. More relaxed, black and white snaps: a young man with a Glengarry trying to keep his wavy hair in place, smiling as he leaned in an exaggerated manner on the bonnet of a military vehicle; and Mary too, young and smiling faintly. The house was a place dearly loved, the well from which they sprung. The last to live here had been a woman with only the ghosts to keep her company in the lonely hours of the night. And how many ghosts there were.

Cal returned down the stairs to the living room. Here, the furniture was fairly modern. The main feature was a dresser. The glass doors housed hidden lights which lit up the crockery, nicknacks and photos, including some of him, one in his graduation robes. An empty crystal fruit bowl sat on a frilled lace cover beneath the display units. A television and VCR filled the corner opposite the door to the kitchen.

The decor was not to his taste, nor, indeed, the design of the house, but its value was in its location, the views. It would all be his soon. And yet, for the first time, he had the feeling that he was losing, not gaining.

He returned to his place by Mary's bedside and time ticked on. Sleep beckoned him constantly and he began talking to her to keep it at bay, reminiscing over happy memories.

'D'you remember that walk over the moor with my mum? It was the last time she was home. The sun was so hot. We all got burnt.' Cal chuckled. 'Remember her climbing the fence and she got her skirt caught on the barbed wire? She couldn't get down for laughing and when she finally jumped the whole thing nearly came off! And those sandwiches you made, oh they were great. We took a break at Fibhig overlooking the sea. What was in them? Just cold meat, I think, but they were wonderful. That bread!'

If Mary heard him, there was no sign. At length Cal found himself unburdening his regrets about his father. The sound of his own voice filled the void.

'You know what he was like. Nothing was good enough for him. He should never have left the island and then he'd have had no one to blame but himself. All that stuff about coming to the city to give me the best chance and that I was throwing it back at him. I never asked him to leave here. This notion he had that being a lawyer was so important. They're the biggest crooks of all! He was a policeman, he should have known that. Y'know, he used to say to me that I made my money by cheating people, that I produced or provided nothing.'

In the quiet of the room, his monologue seemed confessional.

'Even you, his own sister. What did you ever do to him? The way he spoke to you sometimes just wasn't right. But he was my dad and I wish we'd been pals.'

Cal's phone rang, its electronic tones at odds with the setting. He pulled it from his pocket and flipped it open in one fluid, practiced movement.

'Hello?'

'Hi, it's Lisa.'

'Hi. Have you got news for me?' Cal's tone was immediately businesslike. He sat forward intently.

'Well first of all, don't you think you owe me an explanation? Running off like that this morning. You made me feel like a tart. What do you think I am?'

'Look I'm sorry. I told you. It's difficult.'

Cal stood up and walked quickly out of the bedroom, the phone clamped to his ear.

'Why didn't you phone me?'

'I'm really sorry.' Cal tried to keep the irritation from his voice. 'I told you my aunt was ill. I'll be back as soon as I can.' Her disbelief almost poured through the phone. 'I'm not lying,' he added.

'So where are you?'

'I'm at her house.'

'Where's that?'

'What does it matter?'

'Look, I'm taking a big risk for you. Don't start getting smart with me, or you can forget it.'

'Okay, okay, I know what you're doing for me. But my aunt is dying and she asked to see me.'

There was silence at the end of the phone.

'You're consistent, I'll give you that. That's the story you came up with this morning.'

'It's not a story, it's true. I'm in the islands.'

'The islands! They're miles away.'

'Yeah. That's why I had to leave so early.'

'That screws everything up.'

'How?'

'That house. It's like I thought, they want it off their hands. They're here tomorrow just for the one day and I've arranged to meet them. If you get there and I phone to cancel, I'm sure you could persuade them. The usual suspects are sniffing around and you know what'll happen if it goes onto the market.'

'When did you arrange to meet them?'

'9.30.'

Cal sighed audibly.

'I'll never make it for then, even if I got the early ferry. And anyway, I can't leave while she's still alive.'

There was silence at the other end of the line. He could imagine the look of irritation on Lisa's face. 'You've got to understand,' he pleaded.

'No,' she retorted, 'You're the one who has to understand. I've put a lot of time into this and you promised me.'

'I know, but what d'you expect me to do?'

'You've seen your aunt, there's not much you can do for her now, so get back here.'

'I can't leave her. I'm all she's got.'

'Does she even know you're there?' Her questions were coming back at him faster than he could think. 'You've got a choice, Cal. If you don't get back here and make this deal work, you can forget it. I'm never going to help you again. If my boss ever found out what I've done, I'd be for it and you know that.'

The line went dead. Cal cursed savagely. This was the make-or-break deal. He'd studied the West End, watching for houses and flats that could offer a potentially substantial profit, but people were canny enough to know the value of their property. On a tour one evening, he'd chanced upon an elderly lady in a wheelchair being taken into an ambulance. The paramedics were her only company, no friends or family in evidence. He'd reasoned that if there had been any relatives she would have called them when she required assistance. He kept a regular watch on the house and there was no sign that the woman had returned.

Lisa worked for a well established local estate agency and Cal had got to know her through his property dealings. She was an attractive, if rather soulless girl, but he had pursued her ruthlessly. It had paid off. The elderly woman's son lived in London and wanted the ties of the house to be cut as quickly as possible. Lisa had been the one who'd taken his call and she had informed Cal. Everything had been coming together, until last night's phone call.

Cal looked out of the living-room window. All was deep black.

He had come and now he could go. What more could be expected of him? And who was judging him? If he clinched this deal, he would be on his way. 'Look forward!' he urged himself. This struggle between future and past should have been straightforward, but for the fact of Mary dying in the room next door. She was the personification of his past and that made the choice so hard.

He walked through the house and out the back door, following the path round to the front. The wind chilled his cheeks and through the dark mounds of the land, he could see the moon shifting on the sea. His car sat at the end of the path on the other side of the gate. He could just get in it now and drive away. What further comfort could he give Mary? He had come and she'd known it, so what else was there to keep him? If she was dead by morning, what difference would it make whether he was sitting by her? None. If he secured this house in the city, his business would get the kick start it needed. And that's what it came down to: where his presence would make the difference.

He strode briskly back inside to get his jacket. Pulling it on, he went through to say goodbye to his aunt for the last time. The young Mary looked at him from a photo on the lobby wall. Her hair was short and straight and draped over one eye, slender legs emerged from a short skirt beneath a raincoat. Her expression was somewhere between a smile and a laugh and she radiated the vigour of life. The picture was in stark contrast to the emaciated figure in the bed, whose life was rotting from within.

Cal approached Mary to say his final goodbye. He rested his elbow on the pillow and leant over to kiss her, his lips touching her forehead quickly and lightly. There was nothing he could think of to say and he did not want to linger.

He walked purposefully out of the room, through the house to the back door, and stepped onto the path just as Mairi was closing the gate behind her. His intention had been to phone her when he was on his way because he didn't want to tell her to her face that he was going.

'Oh, am I too late?' she asked, concern catching her voice.

'No, no,' Cal stammered. 'I stepped out for some fresh air.'

Mairi approached him up the path, pulling her jacket protectively around her and stared at him. He couldn't bring himself to tell her that he was leaving. For reasons that reared quickly and he didn't understand, he did not want to lose the respect of this good, honest woman.

'Has there been any change?'

'No, she's just as she was.'

They stood together uncertainly, looking into the night, each aware of the silence but neither sure how to break it.

'I'll go in,' Mairi said finally.

Cal watched her disappear round the corner of the house and quietly cursed. He couldn't leave now. She had looked right into his eyes and he knew she suspected what he had been about to do. It was enough to force him to stay. As the night closed in around him, he reflected on the chance that was slipping away.

In the bedroom, Mairi had left the chair vacant for him and had seated herself at the foot of the bed. She was gently stroking Mary's leg through the covers. Cal threw off his jacket and slumped into the chair.

'You'll be tired,' said Mairi. 'You've had a long day.'

'You too,' he acknowledged, bending his head back and stretching his neck muscles.

The silence descended between them again and it made Cal uncomfortable.

'That photo in the hall,' he began, directing his comments vaguely towards Mary. 'That one of you as a young woman. You were a looker in your day. You must have had a job keeping the boys at bay.'

Mairi smiled affectionately at the prone figure in the bed.

'I wonder why she never married?' Cal asked directly to Mairi. He accepted that Mary wasn't hearing him. Mairi shook her head gently, her mouth tightly closed, fighting back tears.

'Maybe she never found the right guy.' Cal answered his own question. 'She's just such a loving person I can't imagine that there was never anyone, but if there was, she kept it to herself. Didn't you Mary? You listened to all that stuff I used to tell you and I never let you say anything to me. Not that I suppose you would have anyway.'

Mary moaned quietly, startling them. Cal and Mairi both leaned forward, their heads close to her.

'What's that?' encouraged Cal. 'D'you want to say something?' But there was no more.

Cal would never know the precise moment of her passing. Her breathing had been barely discernible for the final few hours, but after a while he realised that she had not drawn breath at all. Mairi had fallen asleep, draped across the foot of the bed.

Cal sat up quickly, touched his fingers against Mary's neck and felt no pulse. She was gone. Emotion welled up deep within him for this woman who had always looked for the best in him. His eyes misted and he kissed her softly on the forehead. Now he truly was all alone, the last of the line.

He took a deep breath to compose himself, laid her bony hand on the bed and gently shook Mairi. She woke with a start.

'She's gone,' said Cal gently, failing to hold back the tears.

5

MAIRI TOOK OVER, phoning the doctor, who arrived promptly and confirmed what they already knew. Cal and Mairi hovered uncertainly behind him as he checked the body.

'Yes, I'm afraid there's no doubt,' he pronounced with a sigh.

Cal had witnessed death before, looked upon both his mother and father after they died. What made that difference between the living body and the dead shell? The heart stopped beating and the lungs stopped inflating – was that all it took for somebody to cease to be, or did something else leave the body, what religious folk speak of as the soul?

Generally Cal tried not to dwell on such great questions, but here, with death before him again, they were brought into sharp focus. Was Aunt Mary's spirit already in Paradise with those who had gone before, or was all that she ever was now lying there, growing cold in front of him? Was faith in an afterlife simply protection from the awful prospect of nothingness?

The doctor knew Mairi and was taking details from her

for the death certificate.

'The time of death was an hour ago?'

'Well that's when we noticed.' Mairi looked over to Cal and brought him up from the depths of his thoughts.

'It may have been a couple of minutes before, I could see she was breathing up until then.'

'You must be Mary's nephew?' said the doctor.

Cal nodded.

'I'm very sorry. You must be the next of kin – as far as I'm aware, Mary has no other family.'

'No. I'm it. The last of the line.' Cal's voice caught on that familiar phrase.

'It was peaceful at least.'

Cal nodded again.

'It's up to yourself what we do now. I can arrange for the undertaker to take the body away. Or he could dress the remains and leave them here until the funeral. Some of the older folk prefer to do that.'

Cal looked to Mairi.

'It's up to you, whatever you want to do,' she said.

'I don't know. I wouldn't want to leave her here on her own and frankly I'm not comfortable with a dead body in the house.'

'I could stay if you want,' she volunteered.

'That's good of you, but you've done enough.' Turning to the doctor he said, 'If you could ask them to take her away, I think that would be best.'

After the doctor had gone, Cal and Mairi sat sombrely at the kitchen table.

'Will you be staying?' she asked.

'I don't think so. I'll need to wait until the hotel opens, but I think I'll get a room there. Just, well, you know…' He let his explanation trail off.

'It's probably best for you. It'll get busy.'

'Oh yeah,' Cal groaned, 'There's all that to go through.'

'Folk just want to pay their respects.'

'Or they want to come and look holy.'

Mairi looked taken aback.

'I saw it when my parents died. All these church people taking over the house, having their interminable services. Friends and family were different, but I hardly knew any of these people. I didn't need it, to be honest.'

'It's just the way things are done. It's what Mary would want.'

'I don't know about that. She didn't care much for all that holier than thou crap.'

'Maybe not, but it's what she'd expect,' insisted Mairi. 'It's the way things are done here.'

Cal saw a feistiness in her that hadn't been apparent before. They were both so tired, emotions were not so easily controlled.

'You're right, of course you are,' he said consolingly.

Through the kitchen window the first light of morning filtered in. Cal walked to the door and stepped outside, immediately enjoying the coolness around him. The hills were emerging from blackness. The sun's light diffracted into individual rays. A new dawn, a new day. Time moves on.

He breathed in deeply and turned to see Mairi standing with a tissue pressed to her eyes and her shoulders gently shaking in silent sorrow.

'I'm sorry,' she said. 'It's just the thought of everything carrying on, but Mary not being here.'

Cal put his arm around her shoulder. If he said a word, he knew he too would weep.

Eventually, once he knew he could steady his voice, he suggested to Mairi that she go home. 'There's nothing to do now but wait for the undertaker.'

She shook her head and said, 'I'd feel better waiting until she'd gone.'

While they waited, Cal learned more about the woman

who had become such a companion to his aunt.

'I don't remember you here when I used to come.'

'No, I'm not from the district. I came here when I married. Mary was one of the first people I got to know. I still remember her coming over with a gift and how welcoming she was.'

'I didn't hear her mention you, but then she never did say much about her life and I don't suppose I asked.'

'Well she spoke about you plenty,' smiled Mairi. 'She was always worried about you.'

'I was her only blood I suppose. I didn't give her the attention she deserved, but y'know how life can take over and you don't see it. That's a regret that's going to stay with me.'

'I think she understood,' consoled Mairi.

'How did you become so close to her? You're different generations after all.'

'She was just so friendly. And when Colin died, she was always there for me. She couldn't have been nicer, coming down to see that I was alright, but not in an intrusive way. She would even take the kids over to town to give me time to myself. It was good for them to get away from the house and that was how I got my crying done. I was trying to be strong in front of them. She seemed to understand that.'

'The one thing she definitely never spoke to me about was the cancer. Last time I saw her, she seemed fine.'

'It was very aggressive. As far as I know she was only diagnosed at the turn of the year. Her courage was incredible.'

'She should have told me.'

'Would it have made any difference?' asked Mairi. 'I mean, what could you have done? She thought you had enough to deal with.'

'You discussed it with her?'

'I said she should tell you, but she wouldn't. It was only at the very end that she told me to call you.'

'She told you, or did you do it yourself?'

'No, she wanted to see you. When she knew there wasn't long left, she became anxious. I think she wanted to speak to you.'

He got up abruptly and walked back through to the bedroom where Mary was lying. The doctor had placed her arms by her side and removed all but one of the pillows from behind her head. He looked down on her sallow, lined face and placed his hand on her forehead, pushing back a stray grey hair.

Kneeling by the bed, he whispered softly to her.

'You were special. I never said it, like so much else, but you were. You were the closest I had on earth and now you're gone. I'll never forget you, Mary.'

6

CAL WAS BOTH sad and relieved when the undertakers arrived soon after nine o'clock. He followed them into Mary's bedroom.

'You might prefer to wait in another room, sir. If you'll just give us a few minutes.'

Cal went back through to the kitchen with Mairi.

The undertaker was as good as his word and he and his assistant performed their sombre task with due respect and dignity. Even so, the sight of the simple, dark coffin being carried through the house was startling. Somehow it seemed so much bigger than the small body that had lain on the bed. Mairi curled forward and wept sorely. Cal ran his hand across her shoulders in a feeble attempt at comfort. He followed her to the window to watch the hearse carry Mary away. Mairi turned to him for solace and he held her until her tears subsided.

'If you want to get any rest at all today, you'd be better checking into the hotel now,' Mairi advised as she pulled herself together. 'Word will have got round already and people will be calling all day into the evening. It's a lot to deal with.'

'Would you mind being here to help? I don't know most of them.'

'Of course,' she said. 'I'll need to check on things at home, but I'll come back this afternoon. I'll also let people know that there will be nobody here until later.'

'I'm grateful for everything you've done,' said Cal, suddenly feeling very weary.

The two of them walked through to the bedroom. The sheets had been pulled back on the bed, revealing a shallow imprint on the mattress where Mary had lain. Cal tugged them back into place and drew the curtains, returning the room to shadow. Then they worked their way round the ground floor, closing drapes and checking that everything was switched off.

Finally, they left the house, but Cal struggled with the lock. Mairi took the key from him and clicked it round, jerking the door handle with familiar ease.

'Can I give you a lift?' he offered.

Mairi pointed to a modern house just two hundred yards away. 'You could, but I'd be quicker walking,' she smiled.

They confirmed a rendezvous time and Mairi went off down the road. Cal slumped into the car. He had harboured a small hope of making it back to the city today and possibly salvaging the property deal, but he had to accept that as chief mourner he would be required to play that role over the next couple of days, not just at the funeral. He would phone Lisa to find out the state of play.

His priority, though, was to get some sleep. The hotel was two miles away and he covered the distance quickly, wincing when he heard loose stones chipping against the bodywork of the car. The sporting lines of the Audi looked at odds with the rustic landscape.

He pulled into the car park and walked into reception,

watched steadily all the way by the receptionist, a middle-aged woman who looked as if she suffered no nonsense.

'I'm sorry to hear about your aunt,' she said when he went over to book in. 'She was a lovely lady.'

Cal showed his surprise.

'Word gets around quickly in small places,' she said in explanation.

'Thank you.'

'When will the funeral be?'

'I don't know. Hopefully that'll be sorted out soon. Do you have a room for a few days?' Cal was not in any mood to talk.

A few minutes later he was in his comfortable but anonymous room. Its principal appeal was the view it offered, out over a loch, moorland hills rising beyond.

Cal kicked off his shoes and collapsed onto the bed. The mattress was firm and the stiffness in his back muscles began to ease. He flicked open his phone, found Lisa's name in the directory and pressed dial.

'What's the point in calling me now?' she asked instantly, her phone identifying who was calling.

'It's too late then?' sighed Cal.

'Of course it's too late. They've been in and it's all going through the agency now. It was too late the moment you took off. You haven't a hope of getting it now, not at a good price anyway. What did you expect?'

'I was hoping there might have been a delay or that you'd manage to stall them for a while.'

'Stall them!' Lisa was speaking in an angry whisper. 'What planet are you on? I stuck my neck out for you, and this is the thanks I get. Do you know what this could have cost me?'

'I'm sorry. I don't know what else I could have done. I didn't expect this to happen.'

'You just didn't think Cal, did you? Just forget it.'

'She died, by the way,' said Cal, forlornly.

'Enjoy the funeral,' she spat back and the connection went dead.

Cal looked to the ceiling and breathed deeply in and out, again and again and his eyes began to close.

He was woken by the rattling bleat of a sheep. As he lay letting his senses catch up, he felt his head thump, his system out of time. The sooner he got up and got some coffee, the better he'd feel.

He didn't wash in the shower, just let the water pour over his skin. As he towelled himself down, he saw his face in the mirror looking tired, his eyes red. He dressed quickly and went downstairs to the restaurant, ordering a bar meal of baked potato and cheese. He dreaded meeting so many people he didn't know, strangers who would know who he was. At least Mairi would be there.

There was rain in the air as he drove back to the house. Clouds hung over the ocean close to the cliffs; it was as if the horizon was at the end of the land. There was no familiar faint haze of smoke curling from the chimney. Today, although it looked the same from outside, he knew the house was empty and lifeless. Wind stirred the grass as he walked up the path. Mary had managed to maintain small flower beds of lupins and roses, but the grass had taken advantage of the time she had been ill.

As he walked round the leeward side of the house the wind stopped buffeting his ears. Mairi's technique with the lock evaded him and he had to resort to a brute shove to open the door. The kitchen was cold, perhaps for the first time in decades.

Throwing his jacket over a chair, he went over to the stove and knelt down. There was a pale blue, plastic bucket beside it, half filled with small, broken peats. He tugged open the door of the stove and threw a clump of peat inside. A tidy bundle of old newspapers lay on the floor. He crumpled some pages into knots, placing them among the peats. A box of matches sat on the shelf above and he used them to light the paper, then rubbed his hands, hoping that the fire would take. There was a knack to it that he knew he didn't have. He might have to repeat the process two or three times before he had a good fire going. He wanted to warm some life back into the house.

Going through to the living room, he pulled back the curtains and lit the gas fire that sat in the hearth. Heat surged out. He stood with his back to the fire and cast his eyes around the room. Yesterday this had still been someone's home. A week before that, Mary had still been moving around it, opening doors, leaning on the settee for support, making soup on the stove, settling for the night in her bed. Now it was so still. Had it ever been so hushed before?

There was nothing to do but wait. He sat for a while, looking around absently. The dresser attracted his attention. He might find a drink for himself in there. He pulled open the two lower doors and looked inside. There was a selection of lace and linen tablecloths, some crockery (Royal Albert he thought), a few drinking glasses, a bottle of sherry and a half bottle of whisky, neither of which were full. Mary always had alternatives available for guests who liked something stronger than tea.

There was also a variety of boxes in different shapes and sizes. Some had string tied round them because they were too full for the lids to close properly. Stacked neatly in the back corner were two wooden boxes, one on top of the other. The top one was handsomely crafted. Cal manoeuvred it out, placed it on top of the dresser, and pushed back the delicate clasps. Inside, set in white satin, was a canteen of cutlery, stainless steel with mother-of-pearl handles. The style was old and heavy. A wedding present to his grandparents perhaps? Or had they possibly bought it themselves, in preparation for Mary's big day? The set had never been used. Cal felt the tears press on his eyes again as he thought of Mary and the special occasion that had never come.

He closed the lid again and stooped to pull out the second box. It was heavily varnished, enhanced with beautiful carvings that appeared Eastern in origin. There was a small mortise key fitted into a lock at the front. Whatever was in this box had obviously been of value to Mary. He carried it to the settee and pulled over a small occasional table, placing the box on top. He twisted the key gently and it turned smoothly with a small click. The lid opened easily.

Cal was mildly disappointed although he didn't know quite what he had expected to find. It contained an untidy assortment of typed and handwritten letters, newspaper cuttings, telegrams that were still in their envelopes and some old jewellery.

Remembering the whisky, he went to find a tumbler. He knew the kitchen fridge had a small ice box, but it had a thick beard of frost and he would have been surprised to find ice cubes anyway. He settled for water from the tap.

The whisky tingled on his tongue. He lifted a bundle of the letters, smelling the age from them, and leafed through them haphazardly. They were mostly addressed to Mary or her parents. His eye caught a child's handwriting and with a start recognised it as his own. He pulled the notepaper carefully from the envelope and read 'a big thank you to Auntie Mary for a wonderful holiday'.

There were birthday cards too, and letters in his mother's handwriting. Beneath one letter he found a blue airmail envelope and wondered idly who it might have been from. He'd already flicked past it when his subconscious registered something unusual. He went back to the blue, tissue-like airmail letter and studied it again. It was the address that confused him. It had been sent to Mary, right enough, not to the house where she had lived all her life but to an address in Toronto.

'Canada!' he heard himself exclaim aloud.

Mary had never spoken of having left the country and nobody else in the family had ever mentioned such a thing.

Cal studied the envelope more closely. There was a bold, red 'return to sender' stamp on it. The smudged postmark indicated it had been posted in the 1960s. There didn't appear to be a letter inside. Leafing quickly through the box, Cal searched for any others, but there was none. He turned the envelope over and over in his hand. He recognised his grandmother's name and address in the box for sender's details. The facts were there before him, but he was so confused that he couldn't link them together coherently. Apparently, his grandmother had written a letter to her daughter, Mary, who was in Canada at the time. It didn't make sense.

Cal placed the box back on the table and went through to the kitchen to check on the fire. The paper was smouldering, but the peats hadn't caught. He packed in some chopped wood and added a couple of white *Zip* lighters.

'Having problems?' Mairi had come in unnoticed.

She smiled as he started in surprise, and a stunning smile it was too.

'I'm trying to get this damn fire going.'

Mairi crouched down beside him.

'Let me have a look.'

She reorganised the structure of the fire, relaid the sticks, the paper, the lighters and the peat. Cal was close to her and tried not to look at her, but he found it difficult, taking in the freshness of her skin and the smell of her hair.

'It's all to do with the amount of air that's getting in,' she explained, oblivious to his interest. 'So if we close the door and open this vent, that should do it.'

Mairi stood up and went back outside to pick up two grocery bags.

'I went over to town to get some things for tonight. There'll be quite a few coming.'

She busied herself emptying the contents, cakes and

pastries, packets of biscuits, bread and sandwich fillings.

'Let me pay you for that.'

'Don't worry about it,' she said firmly.

Cal watched her putting the shopping into cupboards and the fridge. Her sexuality was all the more alluring for being unselfconscious.

'Did you ever know Mary to have travelled?' he asked to stop himself from staring. 'Abroad I mean.'

'No,' replied Mairi, checking a bash on a box of cakes.

'She never spoke about being in Canada?'

'No. Why?' She continued what she was doing, but he had caught her attention.

'I came across a letter that was addressed to her in Canada.'

'Canada?'

'Yeah. Come here, I'll show you.'

Mairi followed Cal through to the living room and he picked up the airmail letter.

'What d'you make of that?'

'What does the letter say?'

'There isn't one in it.'

'There will be. It's one of those airmail letters that form an envelope when you fold it. They were cheaper to post.' The blue envelope unfolded to an A4 size in her fingers. The page was covered in hesitant handwriting. Mairi gave it back to him.

'That should tell you.'

As Cal began to read, Mairi came round beside him.

The letter was from a mother fussing over her daughter, concerned for her wellbeing so far from home. 'Be sure to have warm clothes for the winter Canada is such a cold place.' There was no punctuation and the spelling and grammar indicated an abbreviated education, but it scanned easily enough.

Mary's mother spoke of what was happening in the village,

the harvesting of the corn and the death of an old woman. Friends of Mary were sending their love, she said. 'Take care of yourself my dear. Your loving mother.'

Frustratingly, there was no explanation of why Mary was in Canada, beyond a passing reference to her job.

'I was beginning to think she'd maybe gone over to see some relatives, you know the way there so many over there. But she was working. How long was she there?'

'Maybe she did both,' suggested Mairi. 'She might have gone to see family, but supported herself with a job when she was there.'

Cal flicked again through the contents of the box. 'None here.'

'What about letters from Mary to her mother?'

'There were some, but they all had British stamps. She probably wrote them when she was staying with us on the mainland.'

'Well, well. It's a mystery right enough,' Mairi said with humour as she rose from a crouching position.

'What's so funny?'

'Just the fact that Mary has kept something to herself. We all have our little secrets don't we?'

'Yes, but even if she kept it to herself, you'd think my father or mother would have mentioned it.'

'Maybe they did, and you just weren't listening.'

The evening was busy and emotional with the doctor and the minister and the villagers coming to pay their respects. Some he recognised vaguely from years before. All offered sincere condolences and spoke brief words of tribute to his aunt. Cal was the uncomfortable conduit for their expressions of sorrow. For some of the women, Mary had been a life-long friend. This was a sad time for them, and a reminder of their own mortality.

'I still can't believe Mary's been taken from us so soon.

She was a lovely woman, lovely,' was a message repeated in various forms. Cal listened courteously to their whispered words of eulogy.

Later, the minister held a service in the house. There were long prayers and the unaccompanied singing of the psalms. Church elders and some women, conscious of their rank as God's converts, sat on the chairs in the living room with Cal. Mairi and others made do with standing in the kitchen and the hall. Cal would have preferred Mairi to have sat with him.

When the sermon was over, Mairi came through offering tea and plates of sandwiches and cakes. She was accompanied by a middle-aged woman who smiled at Cal.

After all the prayers had been proffered, people began to leave. There were older folk, men and women, in the traditional church garb of dark coat and hat. Others, ages with Mary, were less formally dressed, and there were younger people there too. This was not a gathering to say a sorrowful farewell to one who had lived a full life and whose time had come. There was shocked dismay that this had happened to someone who had so much more to give.

At the end of the evening, Cal watched Mairi walking down the path arm in arm with what he assumed to be the last of the visitors. When he returned to the kitchen, he was surprised to find a woman he vaguely recognised was still there.

'I'm sorry a'ghraidh,' she said, trying to pull on a raincoat. 'I'm forever at the cow's tail.'

'There's no need to rush,' he assured her. 'Let me help you. Forgive me, but I didn't get your name earlier.'

'Kate-Anna. I was a friend of your aunt. We were pals at school.' The final sentence was wistful. 'And I remember you growing up. She was always so proud of you.'

'I'm going to miss her.'

'Won't we all, a'ghraidh, won't we all?'

Kate-Anna leaned down by the side of the table and lifted

a handbag, which she hung from her forearm, and headed towards the door.

'We'll see you again at the funeral,' she said by way of farewell.

'Can I give you a lift?'

'No, that's very kind, but I'm as quick to walk.'

'Just before you go,' said Cal suddenly, 'I came across something today that's made me curious.'

She smiled indulgently at him.

'I was going through some of Mary's papers, just to check if there was anything needing to be dealt with.'

'Don't worry yourself. Mary would have made sure everything was in order. That's how she was, everything had its place.'

'Well yes, but I came across something that just didn't seem to fit.'

'Are you waiting for me Kate-Anna?' said Mairi, coming back into the kitchen. 'I'll drive you in the road,' she said brightly. Turning to Cal she added, 'Well, that seemed to go okay. You'll have known most of the faces if not the names. That lady at the end, Mairead, she was–'

'I was just talking to Kate-Anna here about Mary,' Cal interrupted.

'Best friends, weren't you Kate-Anna?' said Mairi.

Kate-Anna smiled. 'My yes. We were girls together, and old maids together too.'

She was emerging more clearly from Cal's memory, a regular presence in the house, a greeting over the phone.

'You'll know then. About Mary in Canada?'

Kate-Anna failed to hide her surprise.

'Years ago,' persisted Cal. 'She stayed there for a while.'

'Well now,' began Kate-Anna, 'I'm not sure about that at all.'

'You don't remember Mary being in Canada?'

'Well you know a'ghraidh, it was a long time ago.'

Sensing the older woman's unease, Mairi stepped in. 'Oh Kate-Anna, maybe she wasn't there. Who knows? Let's get you in the road.'

Kate-Anna needed no persuasion and made to leave.

'Goodbye. Thank you for coming,' Cal said feebly.

As Kate-Anna moved to the door, she turned her head, but avoided eye contact with Cal.

'She's at rest now,' she said pointedly. 'At peace.'

7

'SHE KNOWS SOMETHING and she didn't want to tell us.'

Cal had remained at the table going over and over the brief conversation with Kate-Anna. As soon as Mairi stepped through the door on her return, he started talking.

'What did she say to you?'

'Nothing. Well, nothing about that.'

'So what's the big secret?'

'Why does there have to be a secret, Calum? Maybe there's nothing to tell.'

'If there's no secret why would Mary say nothing about living in Canada? You'd think it might have come up some time, but I never heard her say anything. Not her, not my parents, nobody. And then her lifetime pal, who must have known and who looks like she's never told a lie in her life, pretends she doesn't remember.' Cal sat with his arms spread open, his case made and unarguable.

'Suppose she was in Canada,' began Mairi.

'There's no suppose about it.'

'Just supposing she was,' continued Mairi, mild irritation

entering her voice. 'Maybe she didn't like it, maybe she had bad memories, or sad ones. What matters is that she didn't want to talk about it. So let it be. That's how she wanted it.'

Cal was too intrigued to notice Mairi's exasperated tone.

'What could be so bad that she didn't talk about it? Ever. You'd think it might have merited a passing mention. Even the mere fact of it.'

'Not everyone wants to blab y'know.' Mairi was leaning against the stove, her arms crossed and her brow furrowed. 'It's the big thing now to tell everything about yourself. On daytime telly that's all there is, people moaning about their troubles. Well, not everyone's like that. Some prefer to deal with difficulties privately, in their own way. And I'll tell you something, I think that's more dignified.' Mairi's face was flushed.

'Okay,' Cal said in a conciliatory tone.

'And anyway, maybe she did tell you and you don't remember.'

'I'd have remembered that. But then, why would she tell me? I didn't even know she was ill. Maybe I could have helped her.'

'Could you?' asked Mairi pointedly.

Cal was taken aback. 'What d'you mean?' he asked defensively.

Mairi hesitated. 'She didn't want to tell you she wasn't well. "Don't trouble Calum, he's so busy." I heard that often. And what would you have done anyway? Would you have come? Probably not. So what would be the point in worrying you? That's how she thought. It was only when she knew the end was close that she let me call you. If she couldn't even tell you she was dying, why would she tell you anything else?'

'She didn't think I'd care,' Cal said. It was a statement, not a question.

'This is all getting too serious and things are sad enough just now,' responded Mairi, lifting her voice. 'I'm sure there was nothing more to it than she'd forgotten. It was a long time ago. And here we are, beginning to imagine some great mystery. I'm already at the stage I can't remember what I did yesterday.'

Mairi set about tidying up cups and plates, carrying them to the sink and running hot water into a basin. Cal remained where he was, lost in thought.

'I'm sorry, I was speaking out of turn there,' she said, clattering the dishes into the basin. 'I shouldn't have said that.'

'Doesn't make it wrong, though. You just said what I know deep down anyway.' Cal rose to take a dish towel from the bar of the oven and went over to stand at Mairi's side.

'It's been a long night. You'll be glad to get back to the hotel,' she smiled.

'I've got some thinking to do.'

'You've been thinking too much, that's the trouble.'

'Why don't you come up with me for a drink?'

'I'm not sure that's where I'd want to be seen tonight. Besides I have things to do at home. But thank you.'

'No, thank you. You're keeping me right in all of this.'

Mairi's hand touched his arm comfortingly.

Cal left her and drove through the darkness to the hotel. It took some getting used to for a city boy, the world confined to the arc of the car headlights.

He dined on herring, the hubbub of the bar spilling through into the dining room. He hadn't eaten the fish since leaving home. His parents had loved herring and potatoes, their Saturday treat. Cal loathed it, the bones, the fish heads stuffed with oats, the salt nipping any cuts on his fingers. The meal was filling and more enjoyable than he remembered, but he still hated the bones.

He bought a bottle of Macallan malt at an inflated price from the lounge bar to take up to his room. The barman gave him a pint tumbler full of ice cubes to go with it.

Only now did he feel the tension in his neck. He ran a hot bath, poured a good measure of whisky over some ice and soaked in the tub. His mind burrowed back in time, sifting through old conversations and episodes for any clue or hint about Mary's past that he might have missed.

There was family in Canada and the United States, he knew that, distant ties with people whose forebears had gone before, but he was sure there had never been any mention of Mary being over there. More than that, when he'd first holidayed abroad with his friends, he remembered her joking that Glasgow was far enough for her. The longer he dwelt upon it, the more convinced he was that her time in Canada was never referred to. Such disciplined silence could only have been deliberate. What was there to hide?

Cal knew he would never sleep if he continued to turn things over in his mind. He lay on the bed and hopped through the television channels, settling on the news. By the time the newsreader repeated the headlines at the close of the programme, he realised that he couldn't remember anything about the stories he'd been watching. The images had flickered in front of him, but they hadn't penetrated beyond his eyes. He had continued turning over the puzzle of Mary like a jewel, examining its every facet. And he would do so all night.

Sleep wouldn't come. Maybe he could find something at the house that might clear things up. He hadn't looked for anything more after finding the box. He pulled on his clothes again and left the room.

A small group of local teenagers were sitting on the drystane wall that formed the perimeter of the hotel. Too young to get a drink in the bar, they hovered in the hope that a friendly drinker might be willing to get them some tins of beer if they gave him the money.

They watched Cal go to his car. In the city he might have been a little intimidated, but there was no air of malevolence about the group.

'That's some motor, cove,' a boy called.

'Yeah,' Cal smiled in acknowledgement.

'Don't see many of them here.'

'Couldn't carry many peats in that,' joked another.

'It's not really suited to these parts,' said Cal.

'Oh, I dunno,' the first youth said as he approached, admiring the car. 'You could get some speed on that out the Barvas Road.'

'Have a look if you want,' invited Cal, bleeping the alarm off and opening the door.

The boy walked over quickly and leaned in, his eyes darting over the console, the steering wheel and the gear stick.

'I've seen you driving about. You're from the village. Mary's house.'

'That's right. She's my aunt. Was my aunt.'

'It's a shame what happened,' continued the boy, still inspecting the car.

'You knew her?'

'Yeah. We all did. Everyone knows everyone here. She was great. When we were kids we'd go to her house and she'd give us sweets.'

'How did you know I knew her?'

'I saw you. Anyway, like I said, everyone knows everything here. And my ma, she knows you.'

The boy was confident enough to sit in the driver's seat, placing both arms firmly on the steering wheel. His friends drew closer, looking in the windows.

'Your ma?'

'Aye, she's been at the house with you.'

'Mairi's your mother?'

'Aye.' He replied as if Cal should have known.

'And what's your name?'

The other boys immediately responded with a deluge of insulting nicknames.

'Colin,' he finally managed to say.

'I'm going back in the road if you want a lift?'

Colin looked at Cal in delight and confirmation.

'Shift over.'

Cal lowered himself behind the wheel as Colin pulled himself into the passenger seat.

'Anyone else going our way?'

Cal didn't give anyone time to answer, gunning the engine and thrusting the car into reverse in a fluid movement. He heard Colin laugh excitedly, but he also heard more stones thudding against the wheel arches. The boy would have seen him wince if he hadn't been looking out at his pals. Too late for the show to stop now, thought Cal, as he whipped the steering wheel round and roared out of the car park onto the main road.

Colin whooped as they accelerated along the straight, the speedometer needle jumping ten miles per hour every second. They swept up the steep brae and almost leapt over the brow, Cal twisting the steering wheel as the road became a series of twists between hill and rock. His foot jumped from brake to accelerator as if tapping in time to music.

At one sharp turn the rear of the car slewed round, but almost immediately held the road again. Cal knew it was the car and not the driver that had saved the situation. They powered onto a straight, past the church and the school, over the bridge and into a tight seventy degree turn onto the village road.

Man and boy were exhilarated, Colin clearly loving every minute of it. Then came a blind bend which was a challenge beyond Cal's driving ability. He took the wrong line going into it and felt the rear go again. He screwed the wheels violently to compensate, but the momentum was too much and the offside tyres left the road, tearing through the grass to spin on air over the drainage ditch. There was a sickening grinding noise as the underside scraped on the road surface, and then the car came to a thudding halt.

Colin thumped against the passenger door and Cal was thrown in the same direction. There was momentary silence, broken by Cal exhaling loudly through his mouth. He jumped and went round to the nearside, his face contorting with apprehension. In the dark, he could see no obvious damage to the car. The left rear wheel was overhanging the incline, but the body remained on the level. He pulled open the passenger door. Colin was rubbing his shoulder and upper arm.

'Are you hurt?' he asked anxiously.

'No,' said Colin, 'I'm fine. What about the car?'

'Off the road. Can you get out?'

Cal leaned over and pulled open the door. Colin emerged, still holding his arm, and sidled along the lip of the ditch. The two of them stood behind the car and took in the situation.

'It looks steady enough. If I give the engine a blast it should be enough to get it out.'

'We could get a tractor,' suggested Colin.

'No. I don't want anyone else involved. Wait there.'

Cal got back into the driver's seat, re-engaged the gears, gunned the engine and jolted back on the clutch. Three wheels span instantly, then gripped the ground, shooting the car forward in a protesting discord of torn earth, stones and scraping metal. He had to wrench the steering wheel hard and stamp on the brakes to avoid plunging off the road on the other side.

Colin ran back up to the passenger side and got in.

'Just got away with that, eh?' Cal asked unnecessarily. 'Is your arm alright? Should I be taking you to a doctor?'

'No, it's okay, just a bit sore. It's okay, really.'

Cal started the car moving again. 'Maybe this is why there aren't many of these cars up here.'

There was no response.

'You'd better not be laughing,' he warned with a trace of embarrassed humour.

Colin shook his head, but didn't look at him.

'What the hell's that going to look like in the morning? My bloody car! These roads...' Cal halted his outburst, realising how pathetic it sounded. 'Your mother'll be raging.'

'She doesn't need to know.'

'No, she's got to.'

'Really. Everything's okay. What's the point of telling her?'

'She'll find out anyway.'

'Who's going to tell?'

'I have to.'

'Why?'

'I nearly killed her son, that's why.'

Colin laughed aloud. 'You should've let me drive.'

'You're not old enough.'

'Aye, well, you are, and look what happened.'

Cal jerked his arm up in a mock attempt to hit him.

'Don't you think you've done enough to me?' the boy joked.

'You think you can drive better than me?' challenged Cal.

'Couldn't be much worse.'

'Come on,' he protested, 'it was a bad corner.'

'That's the thing with people from the city. They buy these flash cars and they're only driving from one traffic light to the next. What's the point?'

'It's more than traffic lights.'

'Oh yeah, there's roundabouts too. No, this is what you want. These are the roads to drive on, single track, full of bends and no idea what's round the next one. That's real driving.'

'Alright smart arse, how do you know?'

'I've done it.'

'You've driven a car? How old are you? Fifteen? Sixteen?'

'Me and the boys drive out the moor road. Getting a car's no problem.'

'You steal cars?'

'No, we always bring them back. We're going to get a banger and do it up ourselves.'

'Whose cars do you take?'

'Anyone's. Family usually. Angie's old man is usually so pissed at night he doesn't notice.'

'But you could get killed.'

'You're right. I should let an adult drive,' Colin said with heavy sarcasm.

'Don't be smart.'

They drove past Mary's darkened house.

'I'm here,' said Colin seconds later.

'I'd better come in,' said Cal, pulling into the side of the road.

'It doesn't matter, it's fine,' said Colin, a young lad again, his cockiness gone.

'Colin, I've got to tell her.'

'Don't tell her about the driving.'

'I'll just tell her what happened tonight.'

Colin walked down the path to the bungalow, then round to the side door and into the kitchen. As he disappeared inside, Cal could hear Mairi asking him where he had been and why he was so late. Then a door slammed and there was silence. Cal knocked cautiously.

'Come in, come in,' Mairi said. 'Oh it's you?'

'Yeah,' he responded self-consciously.

'Colin's just in. My son. You've just missed him.'

'No Mairi, we… we have met.'

'Oh?' said Mairi, her voice a query. 'Take a seat.'

Cal did as he was bid. The kitchen was substantial, with a table in the middle of the floor. The heat came from a stove with a sturdy, black iron flue. Storage cupboards stretched along two walls. The sink sat beneath the only window, which was three panes wide. A pine dresser stood next to an interior door. Cal absorbed all this in the time it took him to sit down.

'It's actually about Colin that I'm here.'

'Colin? He's not done anything, there's nothing wrong is there?'

'No, *he's* done nothing. It's me. I have to apologise. I was giving him a lift home and I went off the road. He got a bump on his shoulder. He's fine, he had his seat belt on and everything.'

'How did you go off the road? Where?' Her words came in a rush. 'Colin! Colin, come here!'

'Down at the bend near the bridge,' said Cal.

'Did the car go over? How did it happen? Colin!'

'It's okay. We just slid off the road and he bumped his shoulder. I didn't judge it right and we skidded off onto the verge.'

Colin reappeared, silent and sullen.

'I've been hearing what happened. Are you okay? Show me your arm. Why didn't you say?'

'Because you'd make a fuss like you are now. It wasn't a big deal.'

He stood loosely as his mother grasped his arm and pulled up the sleeve of his T-shirt. 'See, it's fine,' he insisted.

'It's red. That'll be a bruise. Is it sore?'

Colin pulled his arm away as she prodded at it. 'Course it's going to be sore if you do that. It's fine.' He looked to Cal. 'What did I tell you?' With that, he left the kitchen and disappeared back through the house.

'That boy,' said Mairi despairingly, leaning against the drying bar on the stove as she had at Mary's house. 'He's at that stage.'

'He didn't do anything. It was me, it was all my fault.'

'I don't understand. I thought you were back at the hotel.'

'I decided to come back up to the house. Colin was outside the hotel with his pals and he was interested in the car. Then he told me he was your son and since I was coming this way, I offered him a lift. He knew who I was, so…' the explanation petered out.

'How fast were you going?'

'Fast.'

'On these roads?'

'I was trying to show him what the car could do.'

'Is that drink on your breath?'

This took Cal aback.

'Well, I had a whisky. Maybe two.'

'You drove after drinking. You gave him a lift after you'd had a drink?' Mairi's voice had taken on a tone of rising anger.

'Look I'm sorry, I...'

'Are you mad? The two of you could have been killed. I should call the police right now.'

Cal had no response.

'You risked my boy's life. What possessed you?'

'I'm sorry. What more can I say? If you want to phone the police, go ahead. I can't stop you. I'd better go.'

'Don't you dare step in that car.'

'I'll walk.'

'To the hotel?'

'I was going to Mary's. I'll stay there.'

Cal was relieved to get out of the house and escape Mairi's anger. He had expected her to be annoyed, but the intensity of her response had surprised him. He almost got back into the car, but stopped himself. What if she carried out her threat? He leaned against it and puffed his cheeks in exasperation.

'Calum!'

Mairi had followed him from the house.

'I'll drive you back.'

She had drawn level with him now and leaned against the car beside him. 'I won't apologise for what I said. But at least you told me. He wouldn't have.'

'I'll be fine at Mary's. That's where I was going anyway.'

'Why?'

'I'm not sure. I can't get her out of my head.'

'You don't want to stay there tonight, don't be silly.'

'I couldn't sleep at the hotel.'

'What makes you think you'll be able to sleep at Mary's?' She caught the look on his face. 'You're not still going on about this big mystery, are you?'

Cal looked down.

'You are.' Mairi shook her head in gentle exasperation. 'Okay, let me tell you something. Drinking and driving. That's what killed my husband.'

'I'm sorry, I didn't know.'

'No, you wouldn't.'

'He was killed by a drunk driver?'

'*He* was the drunk driver.' The revelation stung. She stared hard at Cal. 'I can see you don't know what to say. And there's nothing more I want to say. Some things are best left alone.'

8

CAL'S FACE BURNED as they passed the scene of the accident in daylight. Not that there was much to see, except for tyre gouges in the earth. Mairi noted it indirectly.

'Colin says your car is okay. Just some scrapes, he said.'

'Looks like we were lucky.' Cal could now see how close they had come to real tragedy. The embankment fell away much more sharply than he had realised.

Little more had been said the previous night. He'd sat slouched in Mairi's car like a recalcitrant schoolboy and she had summarily dismissed his protest that he had been fit to drive.

'Doesn't look like it, does it? Anyway, that's not the point. You drank and you drove.'

It had taken a couple more whiskies to overcome the delayed shock and allow him to sleep.

Now he was returning to Mary's house.

'What about the funeral?' he asked. 'I'll need to get things sorted out.'

'It's the day after tomorrow.' She expected Cal's look of

surprise. 'The minister and undertaker sorted it out and I confirmed the hotel when I was waiting for you. Mary had it all planned, right down to the coffin.'

'The coffin?'

'She was like that, not wanting it to be a burden. She had a bit put by so it's done right.'

'That's a bit morbid.'

'She was on her own. Never relied on anyone for anything. It was just her way.'

Cal could see his car as they crested the hill before Mairi's house and he studied it carefully as they drew up. He couldn't avoid the incongruity of its urban sophistication against the rural simplicity of the surroundings. Some might see it as flash and perhaps, he was forced to reflect, that was how they viewed him here. He was an outsider and, in truth, it was not a perception he could challenge. He felt much the same. Connected, perhaps, but not belonging.

The paint work on the nearside sill was scraped but there was no significant damage. For the second time that morning, Cal recognised that he had got off lightly.

The engine rumbled as soon as he turned the ignition. The road was narrow, so he had to drive further into the village to find a turning space. On either side, the houses were empty and in states of disrepair. A house not unlike Mary's was closed up, fading net curtains hanging forlornly at the windows, the roof collapsed, with snapped and broken beams jabbing pointlessly in the air. Another blackhouse, neglected and overgrown, open to the elements. This was the real village graveyard, a place that spoke powerfully of the passing of a community. The tombstones detailed dates and ages and words of loss, but the empty houses conveyed stirringly the lives lived by the dead and the gone. The cemetery was where they lay in peace, but this was where they had been born, lived, laughed and loved. This was where the children had squealed, the lovers kissed and the mourning moaned. Each house was a monument to the loss of a family. Here the village was empty, peaceful and silent.

Cal was glad to turn. He was not a sensory man, but evidence of the village's demise was unavoidable and it saddened him. As he drove back up the brae to Mary's house he wondered how long before it too would be a crumbling memorial to a life gone before.

It was cold inside but this time he succeeded in lighting the stove first time. He left the door ajar and sat back as the tapering flames grew and the aromatic peat smoke curled into the kitchen.

His grandfather had raised a family here. His father had been born here. Mary had made it her home. Photos on the wall told of the generations who had lived here. Was this where it was all to end? With him?

It was a theme of his father's lectures that Cal valued nothing because he'd never had to struggle for anything. He could hear him now. 'Your people had nothing, not even the land they lived on. And when, finally, it became theirs, by God they cherished it.'

It had meant nothing to Cal. Home was not a concept to bind him. He had a loose connection to the city, but felt no nostalgia for the houses in which he'd lived. To him they were no more than bricks and mortar to be bought and sold. He'd never had the sense of belonging that was so strong in this house. Even as he'd travelled north for Mary's final hours, he had been enticed by the prospect of the money the house could be converted into.

There would be no shortage of buyers if he chose to sell. City folk looking to escape the rat race only for as long as it took them to realise that the adjustment to the isolation of island life was too great a change. What then for this house? Sold and sold again, or left to collapse in on itself, on its past?

That decision would be Cal's and it was troubling him

more than he might have thought, the prospect of all that he was letting go. Perhaps, despite himself, all that he rebelled against had taken root in a shadowy corner of his soul.

The faces entombed in the picture frames on the walls looked out at him. Their memories had lived on in this house. Mary had known who they were and they had remained alive through her. To Cal, they were mostly unknown. With the loss of the house, they would be left only as names recorded in national archives.

Cal's musings were disturbed by a 'Hello?' from the door. The minister appeared, a greying man of middle age and medium build, his trousers neat and pin-striped, his jacket and vest black, his collar brilliant white.

'Hello,' he repeated, advancing into the room.

'Hello.'

'I know we spoke briefly before the service last night, but I thought I should call by and see that everything was all right.' His voice was soft and unexpectedly quiet for a preacher.

'Seems to be. Mary's left everything in order.'

'Indeed,' the minister laughed gently. 'She would have.'

He was standing awkwardly in the middle of the kitchen and Cal invited him to sit down.

'Would you like some tea?'

'That's very kind, but I'll say no. You can have too much tea. Some of the congregation are very kind, but they won't take no for an answer. It seems like I drink gallons some days.'

Cal sat across from him at the table and paused, waiting for the minister to say his piece.

'As you say, Mary had everything organised. She spoke to me about it some time ago and said she didn't want to trouble anybody. I just wanted to make sure you were happy with that and if you had any questions.'

Cal agreed readily and the minister explained what would be expected of him at the funeral.

'How was Mary… when she was speaking to you about it?' Cal asked.

'She had her faith and that gave her great strength. She faced what was to come with great courage.'

'You knew her well?'

'Indeed. She was one of those people communities are built upon. Always willing, always supportive. A great loss. As you'll know, she was a Sunday School teacher for many years. She had a special affection for children. I expect the turnout at the funeral will show that they thought the same of her. There's scarce anyone under thirty who wasn't taught their Bible stories by Mary.'

'Did she ever confide in you, about her life?'

'Well now, I'm sure she must have, but she wasn't really one for talking about herself. Why do you ask?'

'She never spoke of being in Canada?' Cal pressed on.

The minister looked of vague. 'She may have done, she may have done, but I can't rightly remember that she did. Had she been there?'

'It seems she might have been.'

'Your aunt and I spoke about a lot of things and I don't recall any mention of that. There are plenty of people from here in Canada, right enough. Some in the congregation would know. I'm sure I could find out easily enough.'

Cal let the suggestion hang. Perhaps people might be more open with the minister, if there was anything to tell.

The minister left soon afterwards. Over the years Mary had always talked of her nephew in uncritical terms, but his opinion was based on what she didn't say. She would mention phoning Cal, never the reverse, and there had never been any word of him coming to see her. If anyone ever suggested that he might help with a given situation, her reply was, 'Oh I don't want to be troubling Calum.' And now this man was sitting in her home asking about details of her life. He might have made the effort to ask her himself, the minister reflected, then admonished himself for his unchristian attitude.

Oblivious of the minister's private opinion of him, Cal returned to examining the photos on the walls. On the upstairs landing he heard the door of the guest bedroom rattle and remembered that he had not closed the window. The simple action of closing it returned the room to silence and reminded him of all that had changed in the house since he opened it. Everything.

Turning from the window, Cal looked around the room. This had been the guest bedroom. A double bed stood against the outside wall, tidily made up, covered with a gold-coloured, padded quilt. Above the headboard hung a faded watercolour of the coastline. A dressing table dominated the back wall, its mirror reflecting his silhouetted image back to him. On the third wall was a wardrobe, partially hidden by the open door, which was why it hadn't registered with him before. A tall, substantial chest of drawers sat in the corner between the door and the window. On top was a thin white vase with linen roses.

He noticed two leather cases beneath the bed and an old cardboard one sitting on top of the wardrobe.

He knelt down to pull one of the cases out. It slid out easily. The spring-loaded snaplocks were rusty and reluctant to open. Eventually they flipped up. He lifted the case onto the bed and pulled up the lid. Folded on top was a tweed blanket of thick stitching and rough texture and underneath that another blanket of rough wool, cream coloured with pale black trim. There was nothing else. Cal didn't know what he hoped to find, but the blankets were a disappointment.

He turned his attention to the case on top of the wardrobe, teasing it forward with his fingers until it toppled into his hands. It was heavier than he had anticipated and he nearly dropped it. This time the locks were very stiff and out of alignment. At length, with reddened fingertips and a bent fingernail, Cal had them open.

The case was neatly packed with aged photo albums, shoe boxes and some smaller boxes that looked as if might hold trinkets and mementoes. If there was anythi be found, it would be here.

He carried the case across to the window to get the and sat beneath it, his back against the wall. Outside, wind worried the window. The first box contained cards c sizes and for all occasions. There was a batch of twenty- birthday cards tied together, every one with a gold embo 'key to the door' on the front. The rhymes gloried in the of the future, of freedom, of independence. As he brov through them, Cal pondered on whether the final reflecti of the fading woman had matched the hopes of the flower one. Did they ever? It was so easy to forget that Mary l been young, with unbounded dreams and powerful passio

The second box was more intriguing. It contained lett and cuttings. While the cards marked the events that othe chose to celebrate or commiserate, this second box was wha Mary herself had considered important. And immediately catching Cal's eye was the pale blue of airmail envelopes. Even before he looked at them, Cal knew their destination had been Canada.

9

THERE WAS NO secret any more. The letters told the story. Mary had indeed gone to Canada. The correspondence from her mother followed her adventure, from the first anxious days of her arrival in a foreign land, to starting a new job and finding an apartment.

'Dearest Daughter' was always the opening phrase. 'We miss you so and the house is so quiet with you gone.'

Another early letter asked, 'Are you eating well? Your father worries always that you are cold.'

A friend, Jean, emerged as the driving force for the two girls leaving their homeland. She had relatives in Toronto who had put them up for the first few weeks. The girls had worked in bank jobs that it seemed they had secured before crossing the Atlantic.

The anxiety of the early letters gradually gave way to a more relaxed acceptance of Mary's decision, but the pain of parting was never far away, although Mary's own enthusiasm shone through the caution of her mother's words. 'I wonder about you living in a place away from Jean's family. You are young and your father worries about you and Jean being on your own but if you think that would be best.'

Canada emerged as a nation of aspiration, but in many respects not so far removed from her home country. It seemed that Mary made island connections in all areas of her new life: in work, at dances and the church. The fact that she was attending church brought particular comfort to her folks at home. Inevitably, she met someone her mother knew from the district: 'I remember her so well and the times we shared together as children. She will have enjoyed your stories from home.'

A boyfriend was mentioned. She had met him through the church and he had Scottish roots. Her mother wrote, 'I am glad it is one of our own that is making you happy.'

There were twenty letters in all, the postmarks showing that they had been sent faithfully every month. All were necessarily brief, because they could only fill one side of the paper. As well as questioning Mary about her new life, they supplied news of the village – the work of the seasons, who had been at the dances in the drill hall, people returning for the summer holidays. They told of a community losing its young. 'That is Kenny John away to the police in Glasgow.' Others joined the merchant navy, went to the city, moved to England, others yet, like Mary, embarked on new lives in far-flung lands. No one came back to stay. The ways of their forebears held scant appeal in the modern world. The community's lifeblood was seeping away, drawn by new opportunities, and the land that earlier generations had had fought so hard to secure fell fallow and overgrown. The old folk could only watch.

From the last letter, it was apparent that Mary meant to remain in Canada permanently. 'It pains me that we may never see you again. Your father has gone silent this past while just like he was when you first said you were going. I know the life of the croft is not for you but when you left I always hoped you would return to us but why should you? Many before have gone and never seen the home hearth again.' The letter ended with the usual entreaty to look after herself. There was no mention of Mary's imminent return, no indication of the pleasure of anticipation. In satisfying his curiosity about one enigma, Cal had stumbled across another.

All the letters to Canada were in this one bundle, with the sole exception of the one he had first come across, the one marked 'Return to Sender'.

He heard movement downstairs.

'Calum?' Mairi's voice called.

Cal dropped the letters to the floor and jumped to his feet with an instinctive enthusiasm that left his brain behind. He descended the stairs two at a time and had to slow himself down so that he didn't burst into the living room.

'Hi! I was upstairs.'

'I heard,' smiled Mairi.

'So you're talking to me again?'

'I never wasn't. Anyway, forget that. I saw the minister was here.'

'You weren't kidding when you said everyone knows everything here.'

'I saw his car from the kitchen. Anyway, I brought you some sandwiches. You haven't made yourself anything have you?'

'You know me too well already.'

'It was an easy guess.'

'Well, I've found something you'll never guess.'

'What this time?'

'Canada. Mary in Canada, remember? She *was* there.'

'How do you know?'

'More letters. She worked there for a couple of years.'

'What letters?'

'From her mother, my grandmother, to her. But here's the thing. She came home suddenly and there's no mention of that anywhere in them.'

Mairi's expression was confused.

'The letters are all about Mary's life there and then all of a sudden they stop and she's back here.'

'Oh Calum,' she sighed, 'you're looking for mysteries again where there are none.'

'Read them yourself. You'll ask the same question.'

'I'm not sure I want to read someone's private letters.'

'They're not private. At least, there's nothing very private in them.'

'Still, they weren't written by me or sent to me, so I'd feel uncomfortable looking at them.'

'Oh, come on! Historians do it all the time, they even publish books with nothing but letters in them. There's nothing wrong in it.'

'They're dealing with matters of historical importance. You're talking about Mary's private life.'

'It's just letters sent to her by her mother, my gran as it happens.'

Mairi stood tight-lipped and shook her head ever so slightly.

Cal's enthusiasm faltered. 'Well anyway, the point is, they make no mention of her coming home.'

'So what?'

'*So what?*' repeated Cal incredulously, unable to a understand why Mairi couldn't see the significance.

'Maybe it was a sudden decision,' Mairi said over her shoulder as she went back through to the kitchen. Cal followed her.

'It didn't seem like it. The last letter goes on about Mary not coming home and how her folks are going to miss her.'

'Maybe she changed her mind when it came down to it. Maybe she couldn't cope with the prospect of never seeing home again.'

'There would have been something about that in the letters, surely?'

Mairi filled an old-fashioned steel kettle, put a whistle on the spout and placed it on the stove. 'And what makes you so sure you read *all* the letters?' she challenged him, unwrapping the sandwiches and putting them on a plate.

'They were all together, and I checked the box – there weren't any others.'

'You found one in the box down in the dresser didn't you? That's what set you off on this wild goose chase to begin with, wasn't it? Who's to say there isn't another one lying somewhere? One that explains why she wanted to come home. Who's to say all the letters were kept? Who's to say it wasn't all perfectly normal? The only one who isn't saying that is you.'

Cal bit into a sandwich. 'What you're saying makes perfect sense, I know that,' he said through a mouthful of chicken and salad. 'And I suppose it must look like I see conspiracy theories everywhere. But I can't ignore the fact that she never told me. She worked in Canada for two years and nobody knew, or nobody who did know mentioned it, not even in the passing. That's more than just trying to forget something, that's deliberately burying something, don't you think?'

'No, I don't think and what's more I don't care,' said Mairi sharply. 'And nor should you. If Mary wanted it to be forgotten, that's what we should do. She'd have had her reasons. But to be honest, I don't think there is any big secret.'

The kettle whistled. As Mairi made a pot of tea, Cal considered what she had said. Something had been hidden, of that he was convinced. Mairi was right, the secret was likely to be nothing more significant than a minor embarrassment, most probably Mary's disappointment with herself for abandoning her new life. Many would have questioned a young girl emigrating on her own and she might have felt keenly what she considered to be her failure. Maybe that had made her over-sensitive to any mention of her stay in Canada.

The issue was whether to leave it alone. If there was

something she had wanted to keep hidden, then should it be buried with Mary? Mairi had made it clear that that was what she thought. But the Mary he had known was not someone who was especially vulnerable and she had been such an important figure to him, that was why getting to the root of this uncertainty mattered. A facet of somebody he knew, his closest kin, was unknown to him. Was it wrong to find out in a quest for a better understanding of a woman who had been so good to him? That, at least, was a justification he could openly articulate. Within, though, he was forced to concede that much of his curiosity was simple nosiness, nothing more.

Mairi placed a cup of tea on the table beside him.

'Does this mean you're not talking to me again?'

'That's just another of your silly notions,' she said, sitting opposite him. 'So the minister told you what was expected?'

'Yeah, I had to do much the same at my father's funeral and at my mother's before that.'

Mairi's hair fell to the nape of her neck in a gentle wave. It was the first time it hadn't been tied back when Cal was with her. Her fringe fell forward across her forehead, framing her face and replacing the vital, fresh look that had first struck him with a more sophisticated aspect. There was a sadness there too. Faint, black shadows beneath the eyes, which suggested fitful sleeping. He wondered about her alone in her bed.

'So now that we're bickering like we were married, I suppose I should know a bit more about you.'

When she smiled, the sadness was hidden again.

'There's nothing to know.'

'C'mon, there must be. Anyway, I've got a sandwich to finish, so I can't talk.'

'I'm a mother of two teenagers. That's it.'

'No, that's not it,' Cal disputed in mid bite. 'That's not all you are. You're not going to be a mother of two teenagers all your life. Seems like Mary told you all there was to know about me, so it's only fair we balance it up.'

'I was brought up on the island, married the first guy to ask me out and was the mother of two children before I knew anything. That's all there is.'

'That's a pretty bleak assessment.'

'No, it's better now. The children are more independent, though Colin worries me. I shouldn't be surprised…' She stopped and sipped her tea.

'How d'you mean?'

'His father was the same.' Mairi settled into reflective mode. 'I get angry at the young girl I was. I never listened, always knew better. Colin, my husband was called Colin too – he was the same. Makes me sad when I think on it now.'

'Every kid's the same.'

'I was bright, good at school and all that, and I was all set for college. But then Colin and I got together. He wasn't interested in studying but he was good at sport. And he was the first to have a car. All the girls had a crush on him, but for some reason he liked me. Well that was it, my education fell by the wayside and that's why I am where I am.'

'Was Colin from here? I don't remember him.'

'No. The house came up at the right time and we got it cheap because it needed a lot doing to it. Colin didn't want to stay near his mum and dad and mine weren't happy about the marriage either. We had young Colin by that time. I liked the idea of the city, but it would have been difficult with the wee one and no money. And Colin didn't want to go. He was happy here.'

'Does that mean you weren't?'

'That's what I mean about leaving things alone,' sighed Mairi, dropping her head. 'It just brings things up that are best forgotten.'

She hid her face behind the rim of the cup as she sipped her tea, but there was no hiding the tears in her eyes.

'I'm sorry, I didn't mean to upset you. It was just, like I

said, you know a lot about me from Mary and I thought I should know more about you.'

'Well now you do, and does it make any difference? I get upset and you'll have forgotten it by the time you leave here.'

'Look, I'm sorry. I seem to have caused you nothing but upset since I came here.'

Mairi snorted a laugh and stood up to take their cups to the sink.

'Don't be silly. You've done nothing. Well, apart from nearly killing my son.' She shot Cal a glance. It was his turn to hang his head. 'I'm upset about Mary that's all,' she continued. 'She was like a mother to me with the children and everything. She must have had her reasons for leaving Canada and keeping it to herself. If she wanted to take that with her, then we should let her. She's left you the truth as she wanted you to know it. Why not just leave it at that?'

Cal's attention was distracted by a droplet of water swelling on the lip of the tap on the sink. The molecules gathered until it trembled under its own weight. It acted as a focal point for the daylight coming in through the window, until the diffracted light momentarily became a diamond of brilliant, searing white. Then the bonds broke and the drop fell away into nothing.

10

'ENOUGH OF THE past,' said Mairi, returning to the table. 'What are your plans for the future?'

'I don't know. I'd never thought about it before, y'know the prospect of this house being mine. I thought Mary would be around for years yet. You just do, don't you? So it never occurred to me. In some ways I wish it wasn't mine now. It's a responsibility. My family's been here all these years and I've got to decide what to do with it.'

'There you go, thinking about the past again.'

Cal laughed. 'But you know what I mean?'

'No, I don't. None of these people are here anymore to pass judgement. You're not going to give up your life to come here, are you?'

'It's true, I can't see that happening. I'm not cut out for this life.'

'It's not much different from anywhere else now. We've even got the electricity,' said Mairi wryly.

'I know that, but I'm a city person.'

Their attention was drawn by the thud of footsteps

approaching the door. A large figure loomed through the glass.

'Oh, it's Finlay,' said Mairi, her discomfort was unmistakeable. 'What does he want?'

The door was pushed open without a knock, and a ruddy, outdoor face appeared around it, a lock of burnt blonde hair falling over the brow.

'Hello,' boomed a powerful voice. Seeing Cal and Mairi inside, he removed his head and instructed 'Sios!'

Opening the door wide, he stepped boldly into the kitchen and Cal could see the instruction had been issued to two sheepdogs, distinctive black and white border collies. Both dogs instantly went down on their haunches.

The man pushed the door shut behind him, evidently intent on staying. He was big, above six feet, with a barrel chest that was accentuated by the denim dungarees he wore. The trouser legs were tucked into old black wellingtons, with grey tweed socks visible over the top. Beneath the bib of the dungarees he wore a frayed, brown Arran sweater and the worn collar of a burgundy shirt could just be seen. His jacket was green Harris Tweed overlain with a wide brown check.

'Mairi,' he proclaimed, his tone demanding attention. 'I didn't expect to see you still here.'

The accent was very strong, more suited to his native Gaelic.

Mairi stood up and went to the sink and he sat uninvited where she had been, his legs splayed wide and his arm resting on the table. He was no stranger to this house.

'Aren't those children of yours getting hungry?'

Cal resented his presence.

'What about that?' the man laughed, nodding to Cal, as if including him in the joke. 'Sometimes you'd think this is where she stays, isn't that right?'

Mairi's mouth stretched to a closed smile.

'You'll be wanting some tea, Finlay?'

'Whatever's in the pot.' He fixed his rheumy blue eyes on Cal.

'So sad about Mary. It was, it was.'

Cal nodded and considered re-establishing control of the situation by asking the man who exactly he was.

'So sudden, aye,' Finlay continued. 'The funeral's the day after tomorrow.'

'That's right.' It was Cal's first utterance in his presence.

'Then to the hotel.' Finlay wasn't seeking confirmation. Cal understood he was being told. 'I know,' he said.

'You'll be off after that, no doubt?'

'I don't know.'

'Well that's why I'm here,' he said, turning towards Cal and clasping his hands on the table. 'Mairi, I'd like to talk to this man alone.'

Cal's ire was rising.

'It's okay, I'm quite happy for her to be here.'

'Oh, it's like that, is it?' joked Finlay falsely. 'I'd prefer to speak to you alone.'

'I was just going anyway,' said Mairi, flustered.

'You're only just here,' protested Cal.

'I can call back.' She smiled sheepishly at him, swung on her jacket and left.

The two men watched her go.

'Now then...' began Finlay, leaning forward intently.

'Hold on,' interrupted Cal, his annoyance coming to the fore. 'Why did she have to go?'

Finlay was taken aback, plainly unused to being challenged.

'Mairi's a good-looking woman right enough, but I don't want her hearing what I have to say.'

Cal could only shrug. 'You'd better get on with it then.'

'There was always tea in the pot here,' Finlay reflected, looking round the kitchen. 'My yes, I was here often. I worked the croft for Mary.' He glanced at Cal. 'Oh yes, we had an arrangement. I'd work the croft and she let me keep the sheep on it when I needed.'

'You worked the croft?'

'My, yes. The potatoes and the vegetable patch. Mary helped at times, but she was more for her flowers and the garden. You're a city man, you wouldn't notice, but most of the crofts around here? Dead. Nobody does anything with them any more. Not even sheep.'

Despite Cal's antagonism to Finlay, he could see the merit in what he was saying.

The way Finlay was looking at him was making Cal uneasy. He'd be glad when he was gone.

'I'll pay you a good price.' Finlay said.

'What do you mean?'

'For the house.'

Cal sat back. 'Oh.'

'You wouldn't understand why, but I want it.'

'I haven't thought about selling it yet,' Cal lied. 'I will, though.'

'What do you have to think about? You won't be staying here, so you'll sell it. I'm saying to you, that before you go through all of that, I'll buy it from you. At a good price mind.'

'Well, like I say, I haven't thought about it yet.'

'Look, when was the last time you came to see Mary? This means nothing to you, but it means everything to some of us.'

'She's only just passed away. It's a bit insensitive for you to be looking to buy her house.'

'I know that,' Finlay said in a quieter voice and for the first time Cal sensed vulnerability in the man. 'And normally I would never think of such a thing. But you'll be away right after the funeral and there would be no chance to speak to you man to man. What's the point in involving other people when we can sort it out between ourselves?'

'I'm not going to decide here and now what I'm doing. You have to understand that. I don't even know you.'

'Mary did. She knew me very well.'

'Well that's as maybe, and I'm not saying no. Just not yet.'

'So what are you going to do? Let one of the agents in town sell it to some Sassenach with money? That's why places like this are dying. The young folk can't afford to buy and it's filling up with people who don't even stay here most of the year. Or if they do, they're retired and looking for a peaceful place to die. The place is full of them. And they don't just come, they try to take over. There's not a local accent to be heard on the council. Same with anything round here, full of English accents. You think that's what she would want? Another one of them staying here?'

'My aunt didn't think like that.'

'And how would you know?' Finlay was aggressive now.

'Because she didn't, that's why.'

'You wouldn't know what she thought. Oh, it's easy to talk when you're away from it. Before you give me a speech, take a walk through the village. Listen to the accents and tell me that's how it should be. Your family built this croft. Tell me you want it to be taken over by people who don't care. Another artist maybe?' Finlay clasped his hand to his forehead. 'Spare us from another artist.'

'Listen, I don't like what you're saying.'

'Maybe not. That doesn't make it wrong.'

'Yes it does. The only reason some places like this exist at all is because people have come in from outside and revived them.'

'Read it in one of the big papers, I suppose? You should know better than that. Reporters come up to these islands and see what they want to see and write what they always intended to write. They know nothing. And folk read them and think, 'Oh how quaint.' We prefer our own kind here. I thought maybe you would understand that. Anyway, I didn't come to argue. I came to tell you that I want this place and I'll pay you for it.'

'Well now you've told me and I've told you I'll think about it.'

Finlay got to his feet and made for the door. He turned to Cal as if in an afterthought.

'This is the house closest to Mairi. You don't think she would want someone she knows here, rather than a stranger?'

He clicked his fingers as he walked out of the door, the dogs rising together and turning to follow him. Cal went through to the living room and watched him stride down the path. Finlay was a man made for this landscape. He was, almost literally, in his element. Cal could tell that this was a man who knew instinctively how to make the most of whatever challenges nature set. And as landfall for the gathered winds of the open ocean, the island's challenges were many.

Take him out of this setting and Finlay would not dominate so, but then he would have no interest to go. This was the only place he wanted to be.

During the holidays of his youth Cal had remained isolated from those of his own age, despite Mary's encouragement that he should play with local children. On his visits to older people in the district with Mary or his parents, he was received with nothing but warmth and kindness. It was a different story with his peers. They were suspicious of the city boy and the air of superiority that they projected onto him. For his part, Cal felt out of place and inadequate. On the moor he was uncomfortable near the cattle, he didn't enjoy working with the sheep and the dogs scared him. Soon there was no interaction and he remained almost exclusively in adult company when on the island. Finlay may well have been one of these other children. They were about the same age.

Finlay's dogs followed behind him, utterly obedient to their master. What power did he have that the dogs, Mairi, even Cal himself, had been intimidated by him? Away from this place, that authority would be stripped away, but here he acted lord of all he surveyed.

Cal's thoughts wandered as he looked through the window. He saw the breeze playing with the long grass beyond the fence, sweeping it this way and that. A sparrow flitted onto the white cap of a grey rock and twitched busily before flying off with the wind. Beyond, white horses rode the blue Atlantic Ocean.

Every day there would be something different to see outside this window, from the detail of the animals and birds to the mass of the landscape, all of it dictated by the light and mood of the heavens so open above. It was a place for the soul. He remained there in a timeless spell, until a spiral of smoke from Mairi's chimney stirred him from his daydream. Mairi, the unknowable woman who was already such a support and distraction since his arrival.

He remembered what she had said about the letters lying upstairs. 'Maybe look at them later,' she'd advised. 'When it's all over.'

Cal went through to the hall and climbed the stairs. He would leave it for now, but the question wouldn't go away and he knew he would return to it when emotions were not so raw.

The blue letters had slid off each other and lay spread on the floor. He had left in a hurry, Mairi had been the reason for that. He shuffled them together, but the elastic band that had held them was perished and useless.

He looked into the shoe box that had contained them and tried to rearrange the other contents in such a way that the airmail letters would be held together. As he did so, he felt something thicker at the bottom. It was another envelope, small in dimensions, but its contents bulged in the middle. The flap was already open and inside Cal could see a lock of auburn hair, tied by white cotton thread.

Cal studied the hair, rolling it gently between his fingertips. It was so soft. Whose was it? In all probability it was his own. He was her only nephew, after all. It would be perfectly natural for a proud aunt to have a lock of her nephew's baby hair.

He replaced the hair in the envelope and placed it back in

the box. The movement caused a strip of plastic to slip out from beneath the letters. Cal picked it up. It was a name tag that had been cut. When placed together, the two ends of the cut loop formed a tiny circle. A blue cardboard strip had been inserted inside the plastic sheath of the tag. Written on it were two simple words: 'Baby MacCarl'.

11

CAL ENDURED AN internal struggle as he thought through everything he had found and journeyed towards an inevitable conclusion. He had never seen a baby tag in his own home. It was the sort of memento a mother might keep, likewise the lock of hair, but his own mother had nothing of the kind. Mary did.

He left the letters on the bed and went back downstairs to the box in the dresser which contained the return-to-sender letter. He didn't need to open it, the date stamp was enough. It had been sent the month before he was born.

Cal slumped back in the armchair, closed his eyes and tried to come to terms with the enormity of this emotional upheaval.

'Was Mary my mother?' he whispered aloud, the utterance of the words an attempt to bring order to the tumult in his head. Flashbacks and segments of conversations rushed through his mind, overwhelming any rational consideration.

There was Mary, gentle, kind Mary through the years and finally at her end. She had wanted to see him and maybe he now knew why. He thought of his mother, still young in his mind's eye, comforting him, loving him as a mother should. Contrasting the image of her and the sacrifices she had made for him with the thought that she might never have been his mother made him cry. And he heard his father's repeated admonishment, 'No son of mine...'

If it were true, perhaps he could understand now his father's resentment: he was being required to raise a child that was not his own. It would explain too, his apparently irrational friction against the softness of Mary. With understanding would come forgiveness for his father – or the man he knew as his father.

Cal was starting to feel that his whole life been based on a lie. The possibility seemed to crush him physically. He felt his chest tight and breath short. His face burned. He forced himself to stand and make for the door, grabbing his jacket on the way. The breeze outside was a balm, swathing him in coolness, and the peat smoke in the air was curiously comforting.

Cal strode through the wild grass of the garden and climbed the fence into the croft. The barbed wire was sagging and by swinging one leg over as he pressed down on the top strand, he could actually stand astride the fence on his tip-toes before adjusting his weight and bringing his other leg over.

He set off across the reseeding towards the moor with no destination in mind, just the need to feel the fresh, new air fill his lungs and movement in his trembling limbs. With the physical activity, his heart stopped pumping so wildly and his breath became even. His mind, though, continued thrashing between the wild scatter of imagination and the steady pull of sense.

If Mary was his mother, then who was his father? The Canadian boyfriend? 'I'm glad it is one of our own who is making you happy,' his grandmother had written. Was he still alive? Was his true father still alive? Did he even know if

Cal existed? Or was Mary's pregnancy what had forced them apart? Cal decided he would travel to Canada to meet him. Perhaps he had a whole family across the ocean.

And yet questions kept tugging him back all the time. Everything was circumstantial. The only facts were that Mary had lived in Canada and had returned home, apparently unexpectedly, and that she had mementoes of his birth in her possession, which didn't disprove that she was the aunt he had always known her as. Perhaps she had left Canada with the excitement of knowing that her brother's wife was expecting a child and wanting to share the family experience. Maybe she had taken the hair and the tag into her safe-keeping when his mother died. 'Fits just as easy,' Cal chided himself.

An old cart trail meandered across the edge of the moor, sections obscured by grass and heather. He had a flashback to his boyhood. A tractor bouncing violently along the track pulling a trailer loaded with peat. Cal sitting on top, nervously excited, being jolted from side to side. His father, in the peats in the bed of the trailer, his powerful arms draped outside, smoking a roll-up, laughing amiably up at Cal's discomfiture. This was the life his father had wanted, physical and of the land. His mother, sitting rather more primly next to him, her strong features furrowed anxiously lest Cal should fall, her dark curly hair blowing in the wind. Moving to the city had removed her from this hard life and she was thankful for it. Across from her, Mary, smiling encouragement at Cal. 'You will not fall. I will catch you.' She is young and pretty. He sees that now. Two women looking out for him. And though he tries, Cal can't tell which one sees him as their child.

His eyes were damp when he returned to the present. He followed the track beyond the peat banks, round the edge of the brown waters of the loch, across the flat gneiss rocks, through the shallow glen and leapt the burbling moorland burn then climbed up up the ridged rise of greener grass.

His father had understood this landscape and what had

made it. On their trips to fish the moorland lochs, he would try to pass on his knowledge. And because he was sharing rather than telling, Cal would listen, sometimes unsure how much to believe, but he enjoyed the fact that his father might be telling tall tales. He recalled being told that the island, this bare, wind-whipped landscape had once been covered in trees.

'In ancient times,' his father had told him, 'there were trees everywhere. And they're still there, beneath the peat. My, yes, I was with my own father when he dug up the root of a pine tree.'

Cal did not know whether it was true or not, but he saw a relevant moral to that story. Mysteries, no matter how long they were buried, would always come to the surface.

Finally, breathless and beat, he reached the top of the hill. The wind swept euphorically around him, billowing his jacket. Four hundred feet below, the rollers of the Atlantic pounded the flaxen sand, the white tops tumbling over each other in the final hurl to land.

It was a scene he remembered from childhood, and doubtless his father before him and his father before him, to time immemorial.

Beyond the sea-smoothed sand, on a grass plateau, stood the grey and black marker stones of the dead. This was where the islanders laid their loved ones to rest, on the edge of the land against the symphony of the sea.

It is where they would bring Mary. He promised himself that by the time he stood over her open grave, he would know the truth.

12

'FINLAY'S NOT SO bad, it's just his way.' Mairi sat across from Cal at her kitchen table, her hands clasped round a mug of tea.

Cal had come off the moor straight to her house with the full intention of presenting what he had uncovered and challenging her to question the implications. Why he should discuss such intimate matters with a woman he had met just two days previously, crossed his mind only fleetingly. It seemed the natural thing to do. But he faltered as he approached her door, uncertain how she would react. She had already admonished him for raking over the past. When she welcomed him in, he had blurted out criticism of Finlay simply for something to say.

'He's just very straight and direct,' Mairi countered.

'That's another way of saying he's rude. Who does he think he is?'

'Maybe it is rude, but you always know where you stand with Finlay. He has no side to him.'

'So why were you so uncomfortable with him?'

Mairi's eyes fell to her cup.

'You looked scared of him,' Cal pressed.

'That's not right. That's not how it is at all,' she protested.

'That's how it seemed.'

'No. It's just that sometimes Finlay can impose himself.'

'You're not wrong. It was like he owned the place.'

'That house does mean a lot to him. He was there so often and Mary was very good to him. She understood him.'

'What's to understand? The man's a bully.'

'No he's not, he's just had to look out for himself. His mother died when he was a baby and his father was older. It was just the two of them.'

'It wasn't so different for me.'

'I know, but I'm not sure he ever knew his mother at all. I picked up bits and pieces about him from Mary. I suppose she was like a surrogate mother to Finlay, one of many I'm sure. I'm not local of course,' she smiled, 'I've only been here about fifteen years. Anyway, he was up there often. And in fairness, he did a lot for her on the croft. She seemed to know how to handle him and he relied on her.'

Cal pondered what she'd said.

'Finlay's straight off the croft,' Mairi continued. 'I'm sure he's just shy and it comes across the wrong way.'

'There was nothing shy about the way he spoke to me. It was like I was dirt on his shoe.'

'Well…' Mairi shrugged.

'Sounds like Mary took in every waif and stray she came across. A friend to everyone, even that big lump.'

'She was just a good Christian woman. She looked out for those who were maybe not so fortunate. Children especially. She loved children.'

'And what about you? "Impose" you said. Is that what he does to you?'

'No, not really.'

'You know he asked me if I wanted a stranger living next

to you? He did, like he thought he was some guardian looking over you.'

'Really?' There was the fleeting anxiety again.

'You can't hide it,' Cal persisted. 'You're scared of him.'

'No, I'm not scared,' said Mairi. 'Finlay would like us to be closer, that's all.'

'Closer? What, like married?'

Mairi's expression confirmed the answer.

'You're joking!'

'Don't.'

'You're not seriously thinking...'

'No I'm not, and that's the problem. It's just awkward. But he's not a bad man and I don't like the way you're talking about him.'

'Well I didn't like the way he talked to me. Maybe he plays the sympathy card with you, but not with me. He thought he was the big shot. He's not the innocent he makes out to be.'

'Will you sell to him?'

'I don't know, I honestly don't. I can't say I'm well disposed to him, but I suppose it'd be quick. Would you want me to?'

'Now's not the time to be thinking of it.'

Mairi took the mugs over to the sink. As she did so she glanced at his shoes, which were muddied and wet from his walk.

'Look at your shoes!' she said with mild rebuke. 'Where have you been?'

'On the moor.'

'I wouldn't have thought that was you at all,' laughed Mairi, the sound mingling with the tinkle of water from the running tap. 'What took you out there?'

'I found something.'

'On the moor?'

'No, in the house. I needed to think.'

Mairi turned to look at him. Cal spoke quickly to stop her interrupting him.

'I found baby stuff. I'll show you. A clump of child's hair, a new baby's identity tag. As well as the letters. I know you don't believe it, but I'm sure something about Mary's life was hidden and I think I know what it was.'

'Oh Cal, you and your great mystery. You're just looking for things to back it up.'

'I'm not, that's the thing. The stuff is there. I'm not looking for anything. I listened to what you said and it made sense. And then I come across these things and it makes me wonder again.'

'So what did you come across exactly?'

'Like I told you. A child's hair tied in a bow.'

'Yours, probably.'

'A baby identity tag with 'Baby MacCarl' on it.'

Mairi didn't answer quite so sharply. 'Probably yours as well.'

'And the letters. When you read them, there's no suggestion she's coming home. She's getting a new place to stay, she's meeting people, she's even got a boyfriend and then suddenly she's back here. Her mother obviously had no idea she was coming home. Her last letter was returned because Mary wasn't in Canada any more. And the date of that letter was significant.'

'Why?'

'It wasn't long before I was born,' he answered quietly.

Mairi came back over to the table and sat down again, looking at him intently.

'Are you saying that you think Mary was your mother?' she asked slowly.

Cal looked down at his hands and then met her stare again. 'It's possible. Yes.'

Mairi shook her head. 'Oh Cal,' she said sympathetically. 'You're upset and you're compensating with things that aren't true.'

'Where's the compensation in thinking that my mother

wasn't my mother? That's tougher to take, believe me. I don't want it to be true, I really don't, but I'm beginning to wonder. Seriously wonder.'

'Look at it rationally. Why wouldn't an aunt have some keepsakes of her nephew, especially if he was her only one?'

'Yes, if that's all there was. But there's the other things around it, the letters especially.'

'What about the letters? What do they actually prove?'

'Maybe there's nothing explicit, but something doesn't ring true. Everything my gran wrote pointed to Mary staying in Canada. She'd no idea that she was coming home.'

'So things change. Maybe she just wanted to come home to see her new nephew.'

'I've thought that one through. Definitely not.'

'How can you say? You don't know.'

'What's one of the obvious things my gran would have written about?'

Mairi shrugged.

'If my mum had been pregnant, don't you think my gran would have said? She'd have been full of it. All the details would have been there, every twinge, any sickness, what the doctor was saying. But there's none of that.'

'Maybe with your mother in the city she wasn't hearing all that.' But Mairi seemed less dismissive.

'You can see why I've got questions. Maybe I'm wrong, but it all ties together. Mary being in Canada was never mentioned, and why not? In case something slipped out?'

'Your parents would have told you.'

'I'm not so sure. It's not as if I was the child of an untraceable mother who could be forgotten about.'

'Why would they have taken you if they didn't want anyone to know, why wouldn't you have been put up for adoption?'

'I haven't worked it all out yet. My folks were older when I was born. Maybe they couldn't have any children themselves and when they found out Mary was going to have a baby, they thought that it was the best thing to do. I know there are gaps, but it's not as daft as it sounds.'

'I still can't believe it. *Anyway*,' Mairi said, as if realisation had dawned, 'Your birth certificate will say.'

Cal shook his head. 'It doesn't. It's one of those abbreviated ones. My dad said something about being short of cash at the time, but I wasn't really interested to be honest.'

'Get a full certificate then. That'll tell you you're wrong. Look Cal, I spent many's an hour with Mary and she never so much as hinted you were her son.'

'She never told you about being in Canada either, did she?' challenged Cal.

Mairi glanced away just long enough to betray herself.

'She did!' exclaimed Cal. 'She told you.'

'She mentioned it and she got very upset. I didn't say anything to you because of that. I was hoping you'd forget about it.'

Cal sat shaking his head. 'What did she say?'

'Just that. She'd lived in Canada. She mentioned it after Colin died. I was miserable and said I felt trapped here and she said that going somewhere else was no guarantee of happiness. She said it had been a sad time.'

'Did she say why?'

'No. She got very agitated.'

'All that stuff you said about secrets. It seems it's okay for other people to know them, but not me. And I'm the one who should know.'

'Why?'

'Because it concerns me, that's why,' Cal said forcefully.

Mairi's feistiness returned. 'If she'd have wanted you to know she'd have told you.'

'So why didn't she?'

'What are you asking me for? Did you ever give her the chance?'

'What else do you know? What else did she tell you?'

'It was something to do with her boyfriend. They were supposed to get married, but he called it off. That's why she came home.'

Cal drummed his fingers on the table and then stood up.

'I'm going to go.'

'I'm sorry,' Mairi said sincerely.

'I'm blundering about trying to make sense of things that everyone else knows. You and that other woman, what was her name? Kate-Anna. It would be good if someone was straight with me. I've got a right to know what everyone else does.' He turned again as he reached the door. 'Answer me this. Did Mary ever tell you that she was my mother?'

Mairi sighed and answered quietly.

'No.'

13

CAL WALKED UP the brae towards the old house. Sinister rain clouds now filtered the light down to cast a gloom over a melancholy landscape. Beyond, the playful white horses were lost to the brooding swell of the sea. The rain was in the air now, occasional beads patting coolly onto his face.

He felt keenly he was the outsider again, kept at a distance. He thought a bond had developed with Mairi, but he'd been wrong. It hurt that she had not confided in him and even more so that Mary, his own blood as she'd said so often, had disclosed nothing to him. The secrecy was acutely wounding.

His walk on the moor had helped clarify his thoughts, but Mairi's confession had wrought further confusion. The rain came, heavy and relentless. Cal dashed for his car, batons of water beating him until he slammed the door closed. He leaned his head against his arms on the steering wheel. Everything outside was distorted in the blur of the downpour on the windscreen.

The ring of his phone made him start. He fumbled in his

pocket, anxious to answer it before it went onto voice mail.

'Hello?'

'It's me.' Lisa's voice was a whisper.

He threw his head back against the back rest of the seat and silently mouthed a curse. This was the last thing he needed, although the life he'd left with Lisa only two days before was at least simpler. He had known then where he was and where he was going.

'Hello? Can you speak?'

'Yes. Why are you whispering?'

'It's still on.'

'What is?'

'The house. For some reason they didn't go with the agency. Maybe we could still get it.'

'How? Where are you?'

'In the office, that's why I'm speaking so quietly. They've just left. I've got their number. If you get here quick…'

'I can't. Not until after tomorrow.'

'Cal,' she hissed, 'you've been up there how long already? You need to get the finger out.'

The opportunity was slipping away. Cal knew it, and he was prepared to let it. His priorities had changed since that early morning phone call only two days ago. The man who'd fallen into bed that night with the girl now on the phone was only ever interested in easy conquests and grabbing the main chance. That man would never be vexed by questions of identity and belonging.

Cal recognised he was different now. He doubted everything he had ever understood to be true about himself. And it troubled him.

'The funeral is tomorrow. There is no way.'

'You bastard!'

'You might be right.'

'What?' She wasn't whispering now.

'Nothing. Listen up, have you got a key for my flat?'

'Why? D'you want it back?' Lisa's voice suddenly sounded uncertain.

'Can you do me a favour?'

There was a pause and her confidence returned.

'Another one?'

'This is important.'

'That's what you said the last time.'

'This is personal.'

'What?'

'Can you go back to the flat and phone me when you get there? I need you to find something.'

'Did I miss the bit when I agreed?'

'I'm asking you, not telling you.'

'Okay. Is it urgent, I mean do you want me to go straight from here?'

'If you can.'

'Are you okay? You sound strange.'

'Yeah. I'm fine. Phone me when you get there.'

All he could do now was wait. Cal fired the engine and began to drive, for the sake of something to do. He felt guilty about Lisa. Perhaps there was more to her than he had given her credit for. All his relationships with women had been based on what he could get out of them, usually the cachet of an attractive woman by his side. And he assumed that it worked both ways: they enjoyed being in the company of a man who exuded prosperity and drove a prestige car. They would move on when they chanced upon someone more attractive, more wealthy, more powerful. It was a simple game with a straightforward strategy.

But Lisa was gaining nothing by doing what he was asking of her now. And she probably knew that the prospect of financial reward from her involvement with him was slim, yet she was still willing.

Mairi was an entirely different creature. He had been drawn to her from the moment they met. They had given emotional support to each other. Yet despite that, she had lied about things that she knew mattered to him. It was patronising and it offended him. It hurt, because he cared what she thought.

As he reached the bend where he'd skidded, Cal had to slow right down. Coming round the corner, a dozen sheep filled the road, marshalled by two eager collie dogs. Finlay came into view behind them, whistling instructions, impervious to the rain. Cal had to sit as the sheep filed by, aware of every bump against the car. Finlay stared right at him and raised his walking stick in a gesture of acknowledgement and Cal could hear the stomp of his wellington boots as he passed by.

Moving off again, Cal was soon at the junction where the single track joined the main road. A grocery van was moving south towards the village and he would need to wait for it to pass, so instead he turned north and built up speed on the open road. Ahead, he saw another collie dog lying at a gate by the roadside. As he approached, its ears pricked up and he could see its head fix the car with nervous intensity. He drew nearer and instantly it was crouching on all fours, creeping forward like a hunting cat. When the car came abreast, it pounced, barking angrily at the wheels and disappearing from sight below Cal's door. It was a disconcerting moment, over almost as soon as it began. He could see the dog in his rear view mirror, turning to trot back to its post, content at seeing off another intruder.

The houses petered out and the road curved away into featureless moorland. As he clattered over a cattle grid, Cal saw another single track road leading off through a valley towards the coast. He remembered that this led to the beach he had sat above on the cliffs earlier in the day. It was also the road the funeral hearse would have to take tomorrow.

It ran like a causeway across the moor. Below to his left a small burn tumbled down towards the sea. The ground had been pared away by numerous peat banks, most of them now overgrown and abandoned. It was a constant theme across the island, evidence of the abandonment, but not the burial of the old ways.

He passed a primitive quarry cut into a hill. No rock had been cut here in living memory, instead it was a dumping ground. The corroded chassis of a van sat alongside the rusted remains of a tractor. A burnt-out car lay further off to one side.

The burr of his tyres on another cattle grid pulled his eyes forward again and he saw a handful of houses strung along the road as it fell out of the moor towards the sea.

Even in the rain, the view was spectacular. The land parted into the cliffs and the Atlantic rolled in between them, powerful waves pounding the shelving shore.

It was a wonder to behold.

The road dropped until it opened up into an unmarked, tarmac car park. Only a track meandered on through a gate and round behind a hillock. A small fence bordered one edge of the car park. On the other side of it was the cemetery.

The burn he had seen further inland was now a small river that spilled off the moor, cutting a gully through the sand of the beach and directly into the sea. The graveyard sloped gently downhill, with the more recent headstones gathered at the lower end.

The heavy rain had passed. Cal switched off the engine and got out. The wind off the sea pulled at him inquisitively, pinching at his cheeks, dishevelling his hair. He was as submissive to the will of the wind as the grass and the water around him. He could hear the rush of the sea, although it was out of sight momentarily.

A small gate through the fence provided entry into the cemetery. There was no pathway and he had to pick his way carefully between the stones. Not every lair was marked by a headstone. Some were identifiable only by a small, weather-beaten, cement post with a number cut into it. There was no indication of who lay there and probably no one alive would know without referring to the records.

As Cal reached the crest of the graveyard, the sea swelled before him again, stretching seemingly to infinity. At some point in history, someone must have believed that there was something beyond the visible, and with such belief came the discovery of new lands. With few exceptions, those who lay under the earth here had a faith in something beyond knowledge.

As he moved through the headstones, Cal read the inscriptions, casually at first, then found himself being drawn into the stories they told. There were several military headstones carved with the names and ages of men too young to die. The same information was repeated on many of them. The date '1st January 1919', the dreadful *Iolaire* tragedy.

Here was a man killed in an accident, there a mother in childbirth, this one an infant. The words on some stones hinted at unspeakable tragedies. Others detailed the lives of people who had lived to significant old age, whose passing had been peaceful and whose memory was treasured.

It intrigued him to see how many had died in different parts of the globe, but who had been returned to the land of their birth for their final rest. Canada, the USA, Africa, Australia, India. What efforts must have been made to bring the remains home and what longing to wish for it to be so.

The same names were repeated time and again: MacLeod, Morrison, MacKay, MacDonald, MacAulay, Nicolson, Mac Lennan. This was a community from which the blood flowed away. New names, new settlers were rare indeed.

Then he saw the preparations for the imminent burial. Wooden boards lay on the ground around green tarpaulins, which covered what could only be an open grave. Close by, beneath another sheet, was a pile of sandy soil.

Cal walked down towards it and for the first time came upon a stone with his own family name. He was surprised seeing it before him, written in stone, and realised how rare it was. The name MacCarl was unique insofar as he knew, certainly on the island. He'd Googled it once. The MacCarls seemed to be predominantly Canadian. How they had come to Lewis was lost to history. Indeed, his father had told him that it was not their family name at all: a sheep rustling forebear had been forced to change his name to escape the tentacles of the law, which reached even as far as the western extremes of the land.

'The district of Carloway takes its name from the Vikings,' his father had explained. 'Carl's Bay. The sheep stealer thought it as good a name as any and took to calling himself MacCarl. That's what they say anyway. Mind you, the family has been MacCarl as far back as anyone knows.'

Cal had been only mildly interested at the time and had forgotten the story almost as soon as he had been told it, but his subconscious had filed it away and it came to him now, surrounded as he was by those whose genes lived through him. Even the man's name on the stone was identical to his. It was a Calum MacCarl who had died in 1930 and also his wife who had passed away some years later.

This must be his great-grandfather. He had never thought of the man before, but standing here above his burial place, Cal tried to imagine what he would have been like. He must be one of the silent figures in the photographs at Mary's house, possibly the one with the long white beard and bonnet cap. Cal recognised the names of his grandfather and grandmother inscribed on a stone near the newly dug grave. Mary was to be interred beside them. In a flight of romanticism he wondered whether somewhere they had already welcomed their 'dearest daughter' among them.

With that thought, Cal realised that he was all alone in this world. Girlfriends might come and go and good times would be had with friends, but there was no lifelong bond, no one left who knew him over the spread of his life. Whoever Mary really was, now that she was gone, he truly was the last blood.

14

CAL WANDERED FROM the cemetery down onto the beach. It stretched for perhaps quarter of a mile, the sand smooth as ice, save for the occasional humps of hidden boulders. With the dead gathered behind him, there was no living soul in sight.

How often did the tide sweep in and out unseen? What dramas of nature were played out here without witness? Cal had the oppressive feeling that he could be the only person on earth.

He quickly made his way back to the car, avoiding the cemetery, walking instead beside the burbling brown river.

Back inside the Audi he felt cocooned and safe. At least when he returned tomorrow, he would not be alone. As the car climbed away from the sea, his phone rang again. It was a voice message from Lisa. She was at his house, waiting for him to call. Down by the shore he must have been out of range of any telecommunication network.

He pulled off the road into the quarry to phone her. Lisa answered quickly and he apologised for not getting her call. 'I need you to find my birth certificate, but I'm not sure where it is.'

'Your birth certificate? Why?'

'Nothing dramatic, just something I need to check.'

There were two likely places it might be and he had to accept that Lisa would be able to study his personal papers if she was so inclined. She might then discover everything he had told her about himself was not entirely true.

He directed her to a drawer in his bedroom where he kept his passport.'It might not look exactly like yours, it'll be smaller and squarer,' he told her.

While she was rooting around in his drawer, he tried to visualise what else she might discover. She came back on the line quickly.

'How do you collect so much junk? It's not there. Just your passport and stuff.'

That was disappointing. Now he would have to direct her to a folder of paperwork in his wardrobe, which contained bank statements and bills. She would see that more than a few were threatening red letters.

'It'll be under some clothes at the top,' he explained.

It didn't take her long. 'Your wardrobe's tidier than your house,' she observed. It was probably true too. He took great pride in his clothes, the outward appearance always seeming more important than anything else.

'Flick through all the stuff in the folder. It'll be an older bit of paper obviously.'

'This looks like it,' she said almost immediately. There was a moment's delay as she unfolded it. 'Yes, it is.'

'Okay. What does it say on it?'

'Just your name and where and when you were born. That's it.' Then she giggled. 'You're how old?'

'Yeah, yeah, alright,' he responded curtly. 'That's all, there's nothing else?'

'No, nothing apart from a signature at the bottom. It

doesn't even mention your mum or dad. Were you adopted or something?'

Lisa had confirmed what he thought he remembered.

'Okay,' he said, 'I've got another big favour to ask. The last one, I promise.'

'What?' Caution crept into her voice.

'I need you to go to the registry office and see if you can get a copy of my full birth certificate.'

'Where's that?'

'That place at the West End where they have a lot of weddings.'

'Oh yeah. I was there for my pal's last year. It's beautiful, it really is. They've got this staircase...'

'As long as you know where it is,' Cal interrupted.

He told her the information she would need, including his mother's maiden name, and suggested she take his abbreviated birth certificate with her. He urged her to let him know the result as quickly as she could.

'I'm grateful, Lisa, I really am. I know I've disappointed you over the deal, but this is important to me.' He meant it, and she seemed to respond positively.

'I'll call you as soon as I have it,' she promised.

As he replaced the phone, he noticed the time. This day of discovery had passed rapidly and now hunger hit him. How long had it been since Mairi had brought him the sandwiches?

As he drove back to the hotel, the light slipped away and the moor and the hills slunk back into the gloom. Cal used to be scared of the dark here. Not just the deep, deep blackness, but the sheer scale of the sky above, with stars beyond counting. To stand and stare into the night sky and lose yourself in the hordes of other worlds whose light took centuries to be seen was to realise how small and insignificant was man. It was overwhelming and intimidating. In the city, in the glow of the street lamps, you could insulate yourself. But on the islands, it bore down upon you. Some lauded the glory of night here, but Cal feared it.

The warm, yellow light from the hotel played on the rippled surface of the loch as Cal turned into the car park. He felt relief at seeing human activity. Returning to his room, he succumbed to an all-consuming tiredness and fell onto the bed, removing only his shoes.

He slept for less than an hour, but his body had needed it. As he showered and went over in his mind everything that had happened, it was no surprise. The fresh air had always knocked him out for the first couple of days after he arrived on holiday. Added to that, the disturbed night he'd had, the shock of nearly crashing his car, the people he'd met and most of all, the emotional turmoil of interrogating his own identity. A draining day altogether.

He dined on scallops wrapped in salmon and assessed all the confusing information of the day. Mairi had made him wonder if he was over-dramatising. His doubts were compounded by her reluctance to be candid. His thoughts were disturbed by the waitress.

'Mr MacCarl?'

'Yes?'

'You're wanted on the phone.'

'Me?'

'Yes, sir. There's a call for you at reception.'

Cal walked through the dining room trying to guess who it might be. It was Mairi's voice and he was pleased to hear it, despite himself.

'There's a gathering at the house again and they're waiting for you. Will you be here, or will I tell them to carry on?'

'Another one?' His dismay was clearly audible.

'It's the way of things. Look, you just rest. You've got a lot on your mind.'

'No, I should be there. Give me ten minutes.'

Cal abandoned what was left of his dinner and returned to

his room, cursing that his day was not over yet.

It took him slightly more than ten minutes to get to Mary's, and longer still to park the car. A line of other vehicles were pulled into the side of the road outside the house.

The lights were on and he could see movement inside. Mairi must have opened it up and welcomed people. Should he have known, should she have told him? He came through the back door. A knot of people were standing in the kitchen talking quietly among themselves. One or two smiled at him, kind, warm faces that he knew he had seen before in Mary's company. Among them was Kate-Anna.

Mairi came straight to him.

'I'm sorry,' she said, 'I thought you knew to come. The minister is waiting for you. He's fine.'

The atmosphere in the living room was altogether colder. The people there were unsmiling and clad in the clothes of the church. Two women sitting on the settee were wearing hats. Cal had seen them for the first time at the service the night before, when they had occupied the same positions. The men were in sombre suits and two still had their coats on. The minister rose from a chair by the window.

'Ah, Calum,' he said, proffering his hand.

'I'm sorry,' Cal said. 'I hadn't realised.'

'You must forgive us our ways.'

Most of the elders now nodded and smiled. One of the women, though, her greying hair pinned into a tight bun beneath her hat, continued to look at him sternly. He disliked her already. Why was she sitting so prominently in Mary's room? Why was Kate-Anna not here, or Mairi?

A seat near the door had been left empty and Cal understood that it was meant for him. The minister lifted his Bible. Looking around the room he said, 'Shall we begin?'

He led the prayers and read two passages from the Bible. One of the elders led the psalm singing.

It was over within the hour and folk began to disperse.

The minister asked him if he was prepared for the following day and encouraged him to call if he had any concerns. As Cal stood at the back door he saw Mairi and Kate-Anna talking at the far end of the kitchen. Eventually it was only the three of them left.

Mairi went through to the living room, indicating with a movement of her head that Cal should follow. The older woman stayed behind in the kitchen, pulling on her coat.

'We need to talk,' said Mairi as she returned the chairs to their original positions. 'Will you still be here after I take Kate-Anna home?'

'I'll take her,' said Cal. 'It's on the road to the hotel anyway, isn't it?'

'Don't be daft. I'll do it.'

'I want to do it. I want to speak to her.'

Mairi hesitated. 'Well, I'll ask her.'

'No, tell her. Tell her I'm taking her.'

'What are you going to do now, Cal?' Mairi's tone was despairing.

'Maybe somebody will tell me the truth.'

'Oh Cal, will you not just let things lie?' Mairi pleaded. 'I'm sorry I wasn't open with you, but that's no reason to think anything sinister is going on.'

'Just let me speak to Kate-Anna. You owe me that.'

Mairi shook her head. 'I can only ask. If she doesn't want to go with you, I can't make her.'

The last chair was back in place and the fire had been turned off. Cal waited for Mairi to go back through to the kitchen and then switched off the lights.

'Calum's going to take you home if that's okay,' Mairi informed Kate-Anna.

She looked at Mairi in surprise.

'It's on my way to the hotel,' Cal chipped in.

'Of course, well that would be very kind,' Kate-Anna said after a moment. 'I don't want to be a bother to anyone.'

'It's no bother,' Cal reassured her.

Just as he started to follow her out, Mairi asked quietly, 'Do you have a suit for tomorrow?'

Cal stopped dead. In the rush to leave the Edinburgh flat, he had thrown only a change of clothes into his holdall. Mairi must have guessed.

'Don't worry. I still have a suit of Colin's. It might not be quite the style you're used to, but it should fit. Come to the house in the morning.'

Cal smiled in gratitude and thanked her. His resentment was going and the warmth was back.

The moon was out, dappling the sea and tracing a luminous trail along the road. Silhouetted against it was Kate-Anna.

This woman knew. And if Cal could persuade her to tell, finally he would know too.

15

CAL WALKED KATE-ANNA down to his car. To start the conversation, he apologised he was parked so far from the house.

'Yes, there was a lot came.' She spoke with the same strong accent as Mary. 'And there'll be more tomorrow.'

She was ages with Mary and wore a plain, navy raincoat over a dark jumper, skirt and flat shoes. She took off her hat as they walked. 'I only use this for the church,' she explained.

When they were getting into the car she misjudged the position of the seat and fell back with a small thud.

'I'm not used to seats being so low,' she laughed embarrassedly. Then she struggled to find the catch for the seatbelt. 'I'm not doing very well, am I?'

Cal tried to help, but it was an awkward situation and he didn't want to pull the belt from her. Eventually she found it and sat back, clasping her hands on her lap.

'I'm not used to these things,' she said.

'You're fine,' Cal reassured her, starting the engine and pulling away.

As they passed the house, Mairi appeared walking down the path and waved.

'She's a lovely girl,' said Kate-Anna.

'Yes,' agreed Cal. 'She's been a great help.'

'And she was to Mary as well.'

Kate-Anna looked at the dashboard as Cal drove. 'Well, this is a lovely car,' she observed.

'I'm not sure how suited it is to these roads though.'

'This is really very good of you.'

'Not at all. It's on my way.'

Cal agitated about how to broach the issue of Mary's past. Kate-Anna had made it clear the night before that the subject was not up for discussion.

For some moments they sat in silence, swaying gently in unison from side to side with the motion of the car.

'I'm just at the cut off,' Kate-Anna said. 'You can drop me there.'

Cal knew the opportunity was best taken while she was in the car. Outside, she could walk away.

'I would really like to talk to you. About Mary. I know what you said, but there are things I need to know and I think you know what they are.' He glanced earnestly at her.

Kate-Anna sat for some moments and it was a relief to Cal when she spoke.

'I'll answer anything you want to ask as best I can.' She directed him to her house, a single-storey cottage with barrels of flowers set on either side of the front door. 'Come in for some tea.'

Cal had to help her release the seatbelt.

'Thank you,' she chuckled. 'I'd still have been here in the morning if I'd had to do it myself.' He was encouraged by her humour.

Force of habit made him click the remote alarm as they went through the gate to the house. The car bleeped and the hazard lights flashed.

'Oh you'll not need to do that here,' she said. 'There's not a soul will pass by here tonight.'

Kate-Anna walked through her front door without using a key. They went into her living room and she switched on a coal-effect electric fire. It was a tidy room with furniture that, although not old-fashioned, was certainly dated. 'Take a seat and I'll get the tea,' she said removing her coat.

It was already comfortably warm. Cal noticed a central heating radiator below the front window. The electric fire was superfluous, but the tradition of sitting around a glowing fire was hard to let go.

'The peat fire was getting too much,' Kate-Anna said from the kitchen. 'It's such a lot of work.'

'I can imagine,' Cal acknowledged. 'At first I couldn't get the stove back at Mary's to light.'

She laughed. 'There's a knack to it.'

Cal looked around. A framed seascape print hung above the fireplace and there were some black and white photographs among the contemporary colour photos of family groups.

'That's my nieces and nephews and their families,' Kate-Anna explained as she came back through with the tea on a tin tray. There was a plate of chocolate biscuits, shortbread and buttered gingerbread.

'Help yourself to milk and sugar,' she encouraged, sitting on the edge of the chair next to the fire. 'So what is it you would like to know?'

'Last night you told me you had grown up with my aunt, that you'd been best friends all your life.'

'We were.'

'There are things she'll have told you that maybe she didn't say to anyone else.'

Kate-Anna nodded. 'Yes, she told me a lot over the years. And me her.'

'You said to let the past rest.'

She nodded vigorously.

'I understand why you would say that, but I don't think this is just about the past. This is about me.'

A quizzical look came over Kate-Anna's face.

'I know that Mary lived in Canada.' For added emphasis Cal repeated, 'I know that. I've seen the letters my gran wrote to her.'

'Well, these letters will probably tell you as much as I can.'

'Not really. They raise more questions than anything else.'

Kate-Anna took a sip of tea and looked down at the cup, holding it to her lap.

'Yes,' she began, 'she went to Canada when she was young. Her and a friend. And you know, in those days that was quite a thing for a girl to do. But that was Mary.'

'Why did she go?'

'Why does anyone do something like that? The island life isn't suited to everyone.'

'I thought she always loved it here?'

'I suppose she did, but you know what it's like when you're young. Life is a big adventure. I'm not sure she'd have thought about it on her own, but her friend was keen to go and Jean had family there.'

'Do you remember her going?'

'Oh my, yes. Well I remember her leaving here for Glasgow. Crying like two children we were. I didn't know that I would ever see her again. And she was telling me that I would come over to see her in Toronto.'

Now that she had overcome her reluctance to talk, the story began to spill from Kate-Anna. 'Oh and her mother was so upset, and your grandfather, well, he hardly said anything. He didn't want her to go, didn't think it was right for a girl of her age. But in fairness to him, he didn't try to stop her. Your own father, her brother, oh now he was different.'

'My father tried to stop her going?

'Your father was very like your grandfather, very straight,

very traditional. You know that yourself, I'm sure. He told Mary not to go. He used to do that, tell her what to do. He was that bit older, of course. Yes, he said she shouldn't be going so far on her own.'

'But she went anyway?' smiled Cal, thinking of the side to her character that he had not known.

'She was an independent girl.'

'Did you hear from Mary when she was over there?'

'Oh yes, we wrote all the time. And she loved Canada. She missed home, but there was no talk of coming back. Of course there were so many Scots over there, Lewis folk as well, so she wasn't so lonely. She was working in a bank and she and Jean shared a flat. Oh, but she was having such a good time and she kept asking me to go over too.'

'So what happened? Why did she come back?'

Kate-Anna looked sharply at him.

'But you know why.'

'She got pregnant didn't she?'

Kate-Anna's mouth crumpled as she pressed her lips together to control her emotions. For a moment she could only nod her head.

'It's the age-old story,' she sighed at last. 'He was a Canadian, a handsome boy. She met him at a dance I think, and she fell for him hard. He seemed to know how to sweep her off her feet. His father had a business, the family must have had money, but that's not why Mary went with him. There was more to her than that. She said they had fun together and he was good to her. I think she thought they would get married. They certainly talked about it.'

'What was his name?'

'Brian. Brian something, I can't quite remember. He was tall and dark. She sent me a photo of them together and he had a look about him that was so different from the boys at home.'

'A photo?' asked Cal eagerly.

'Yes, but I don't have it any more. I gave it back to her when she came home. She asked me to.'

Cal couldn't keep the disappointment from his face. Perhaps he might find it back at the house. Would he be able to see the man who might be his father?

'So what happened?' he prompted.

'What happens so often. She fell pregnant by him.' Kate-Anna paused for a time and started again on a different tack. 'You might remember a sensible, respectable woman, but she was young once. We all were. Young and passionate. At that age when someone special comes into your life they become everything to you and you can't think right without them. You do anything to make them happy. And sometimes that is stronger than the fear of doing wrong. Well that's what happened to Mary.'

'What did she tell you about it?'

'Nothing. I didn't know until she came home.'

'Why did she come back?'

'Because he left her.'

Cal hung his head.

'He told her that she couldn't have the baby. He said he would lose everything. His father would disown him. A story as old as the hills.' She placed her teacup on the table. 'Well, Mary said no. She told him the there was no way she would get rid of the baby and so he left her. He told her he didn't want to see her again. Well of course she had to leave her job and she had no family in Canada herself. So she came home.'

'With the baby?'

'I believe so. I never knew about the baby until after she'd come home. First she went to Glasgow for some months. I've always thought the baby must have been born there. Mary never said exactly when.'

'But you must know.'

'I don't. I only ever heard this years later. At first Mary just said she'd come home because she'd broken up with Brian and had been very upset and homesick. It was only later when there was word that Jean was coming back for a visit that she told me, because she thought I would find out. Anyway, Jean never came. But Mary wouldn't talk about the baby or anything. It was too painful for her and so I didn't ask.' Kate-Anna was dabbing her eyes with a paper handkerchief.

'So you don't know what became of the baby?'

'No, I don't. Mary once said that she still saw the child from time to time, but, of course, she couldn't say who she was to her. That was very hard for her.'

Cal sat back in his seat and sighed.

'I do know that no good came of Brian.' Kate-Anna continued. 'Mary must have heard through Jean. It sounds like he took to the drink and died young. A car crash I believe. She never said much. It was all so, so sad. You can understand why she just wanted to forget about it.'

'Do you think it's at all possible that I was that baby? That I was Mary's son?' Kate-Anna looked taken aback, but she listened intently as Cal explained his reasoning. 'I need to know when I'm at that graveside tomorrow if I'm burying the woman who was my mother. If you know, please tell me.'

'Calum, if I knew, then I promise you I would say. But I don't. I know Mary had a baby. But where it is, or who it is, I honestly don't know.'

16

THEY CONTINUED TALKING into the night. Kate-Anna described a Mary with whom he was unfamiliar. A woman who spurned the many suitors. Only one had ever been allowed to come close, and that relationship had ended in a broken engagement. 'She said that she wasn't doing right by him. He was a good man, but she didn't love him and never could.'

'Why? Did she still love Brian, despite what he did to her?'

'I think so. What he did was bad but he was young and from what I can gather, his father was a difficult man. It probably wasn't his choice. Who knows, maybe he might have come back to her when he became his own man, but that wasn't to be.'

'So she was holding out hope for him?'

'There were women here, old women, who lost their loved one in the wars and never loved again. There was only the one for them and he was gone forever. But that wasn't Mary. It was more that she'd had her adventure and it turned out bad.'

It had been such a waste, Kate-Anna said, Mary would have been a wonderful mother. She had adored children. She had caught her occasionally lost in wistful thought that hinted at deep sadness, never acknowledged. Kate-Anna didn't know whether Mary had ever wanted to leave the island again. Even if she had, circumstances changed and the chance was gone. Her father never recovered from what he saw as his daughter's shame and her mother ailed after him. Whatever the motivation, guilt, duty or simply love, Mary had remained at home to care for her and by the time she was gone, she herself was of an age that limited prospects.

Cal's mother had died around the same time as Mary's. Frayed threads wove together in his mind. When Mary had come to the city to stay with him and his father, it had ostensibly been to help support them. Thinking on it now, perhaps it had been to play the role that life had denied her, the chance to be mother to her son. But Cal had simply wanted his meals cooked and his laundry done. They had enjoyed each other's company, but he had not recognised any connection tighter than what had gone before. His father had made it impossible anyway, with the resentment he bore like an open sore. Cal and his father had weighed her down with their domestic demands and the tension between them. Twice, it seemed, Cal had been the cause of her ambitions being dashed, yet she had shown him nothing other than love and devotion.

Kate-Anna showed him photos that took the two young classmates through adolescence into young adulthood, then on to middle age and finally to one taken just a few months before, at New Year. 'It seems barely any time ago. That was the first I knew she wasn't well. And it was only by asking. Mary would not have said.'

'Why is that?' he asked. 'Why say nothing about these things?'

'That's just how she was, and her people before her. It's like that here. It's hard to keep your privacy, because everyone knows what's happening with everyone else. Everything is noticed. And because it's hard, people sometimes become secretive. But knowing Mary, I just think she didn't want a fuss. She dealt with it on her own and that was just her way.' Kate-Anna's voice wavered tearfully as she continued. 'About two months ago it was clear she was losing too much weight. And she kept going over to town with Mairi. My, but that girl's been good to her. She couldn't keep it hidden for ever.'

'And how was she?'

'Very... What's that word? Stoical, that's it. She just accepted it was her time.'

'And did she say anything more to you about seeing her child?'

'No.'

It was very late when Cal finally left. Kate-Anna had stood in the doorway waving him off. Now he sat at the window of his room, whisky in hand, looking out over the loch. He was not who he thought he was. There were those who said it wasn't where you were from that mattered, but where you were going. He didn't believe that. The two were not mutually exclusive. You are what you are, he thought, and, although that should not limit what you become, it must inform it.

Three days ago he would have been thrilled to think he might be related to a wealthy Canadian family. It would have seemed the answer to all his problems. He would have dreamt of flying the Atlantic and presenting himself before a gathering of the family and announcing to them that he was the lost son of their lost brother, Brian. And they would welcome him with tears and emotion, thankful that all the hurt and shame was in the past and that Brian had come back to them, in a way. And he would be accepted as one of their own and would share in their wealth and be given a place in the family business, whatever it was. Oh, he could have dreamed that readily enough.

For now, he felt nothing but sadness. The excitement of

having a new family might return, but for the moment he dwelled upon the love and passion of two young people and the tragedy it had wrought.

The truth was bitter. A young man denied his love, a young woman cast away and a child left rootless and hollow. And for what? Respectability? Snobbery? But then, what might a father do if he didn't understand and believed his son, in whom he had invested so much, was throwing his life away on some girl? Maybe his motivation had been love also.

Fate had brought these two young people together, they had fallen in love and the result had been wretched, lives spoiled and chances lost. And it would linger on through him as he wondered what might have been.

Tomorrow, in a graveyard where the land met the ocean, should he stand up and proclaim Mary as his mother? The thought unnerved him. Cal reflected back down the years to a day when the rain poured down from weeping skies and ran down his neck and into his shoes. That day, too, he thought he had been standing over the coffin of his dead mother. She had given him unconditional love and her loss left him bereft. He remembered that day like no other because, until that moment, she was still physically tangible. Her spirit was gone, but he could have held her hand if he wanted, cold though it might be. When she went into the ground, that was all gone. Nothing was left. As the lumps of mud rapped on the coffin lid, he had been cut adrift.

And tomorrow. Tomorrow he must go through it all again.

17

IT WAS A night of disturbed dreams. Faces, real and imagined, scenarios unsettling, congregated in Cal's subconscious.

By the darkest hour, night sweats made sleeping impossible. He pulled himself from his bed and poured another whisky, then sat at the window and looked again into the blackness.

This had been the hour of anticipation when he was a boy. It was the start of the journey, either for the train from the city or the early boat from the island. It was an hour unseen and unknown at any other time of the year.

And he knew that if he stepped outside he would shiver, regardless of the temperature. It was the tremble of expectation. Today would be the start of another journey for him, the voyage to discover who he really was.

The water of the loch lapped onto the shore. Everything else was silent and still in the dark. Then came a faint hiss in the distance that grew to the rush of a car on the road, the headlights sweeping past then fading away to nothing again. Another one for the early ferry.

The whisky filtered through to his anxious mind and he

fell asleep in the chair.

He was woken by the crowing of a cockerel somewhere out of sight. Today would be a day of firsts and lasts. When again would he ever be roused from sleep by the king of the dawn birds?

A grey light felt its way across the shadows, bringing form and detail to the land and the loch.

His interrupted sleep and troubled thoughts had left Cal feeling tired and fuzzy. He made straight for the shower. The water sprayed across his head and torso and forced life into his dulled nerves. He didn't allow time to push him on, remaining beneath the massaging water until his body was soft and red.

The face looking back from the shaving mirror was puffy and lined. As he studied it, he identified features that he had never recognised before. The shape of his eyes was like Mary's, and his nose was a masculine version of hers. But what of his brown hair that could turn blonde in the sun? So unlike the dark hair that ran in what he knew of as family. Was it the Canadian in him?

He shaved carefully and the process seemed to tighten his skin. When he returned to the bedroom, he felt refreshed and ready to face what was to come.

The thought of wearing Colin's clothes made him uncomfortable, but it was practical sense. Driving over to town to try to get a suit there would mean cutting things fine and there would no certainty of finding one.

Porridge and milk in the dining room put a lining in his stomach to last the day. The furniture was laid out differently from previous days and he realised it was in preparation for the funeral purvey later in the morning.

'I hope it goes well,' the receptionist said gently to him. An old dog seated at the door stood up lamely as he left. The black of her coat was greying and the eyes were dull. He clapped her on the head and rubbed her side and it was as if she smiled up at him. Then, satisfied, she settled back down in her berth.

A sheep watched him as he walked across the car park. Birds chirped and sang and a family of ducks flurried across the water's surface when the car engine growled into life.

Black clouds were gathering on the horizon like an invading army. It was going to be very wet. Cal arrived at Mairi's house just before the rain, but it would be upon them before he left, of that he was sure.

'Come in, come in,' she greeted him.

Colin was seated at the breakfast table in T-shirt and shorts, his hair all tangled, obviously just out of bed and embarrassed to see someone in the house so early. He nodded an acknowledgment. Across from him was a girl Cal hadn't seen before. She was about thirteen, with a perfect complexion and her hair tied back in a ponytail. The resemblance to her mother was evident.

'Emma, this is Cal,' Mairi introduced them.

Emma smiled shyly and then she and her brother left the table and disappeared through to the back of the house.

'They are going to the funeral. They want to. I'm worried it might be a bit much for Emma at her age,' said Mairi.

'If they want to go, it's hard to stop them.'

'They both thought the world of Mary.' Mairi made an effort to hold back the tears. 'How did you get on with Kate-Anna last night?'

'She had a lot to tell. And I was right. It looks like everything I told you was true.'

'Such as?' asked Mairi, sitting at the table.

'Mary was in Canada and she had a baby.'

'In Canada?'

'Kate-Anna thinks the baby was born in Glasgow and that Mary gave it away before she come home.'

'Gave it away?'

'Had it adopted.'

'And Kate-Anna told you this?'

'She was sure about the baby being born, but not so sure of the rest of it.'

'What else did she say?'

'That was about all. Mary had written to her from Canada.'

'Did she say where the baby was?'

'Kate-Anna didn't know.'

Mairi sighed.

'Mary goes to Canada. She falls in love with a guy and she gets pregnant. The guy dumps her because of pressure from his family. She comes home, has the kid, knows she can't bring it up herself and gives it to somebody who can. You can see how it all comes together.'

'Yes,' admitted Mairi.

'That's why Mary wanted to see me when she was dying. She wanted to tell me.'

'There must be ways of knowing for sure. Your birth certificate, that kind of thing.'

'I've got somebody checking it out for me. I'll know by the time of the funeral. I want to know for sure if I'm burying my real mother. You live all your life believing something to be true and then you find out it's not. That's what I mean about secrets. Wouldn't it be better to know?'

'Not always,' said Mairi. 'And what if you're wrong? How would you feel then?'

'I'm sure. I know you doubt it, but it's true.'

'D'you want to try on this suit then?' Mairi changed the subject. 'I've laid it out on my bed, if that's okay. Just at the end of the hall. Colin and Emma are in the other rooms.'

The scents and decor of her bedroom were purely feminine and Cal imagined her there, despite himself. Bottles of perfume, cans of spray and pots of cream cluttered the surface of the vanity bureau. A hairdryer lay on the floor. The only masculine intrusion was the black suit, white shirt and black tie lying on the bed. Cal quickly swapped trousers. Mairi had correctly estimated that he and her late husband were about the same height. However, there was at least an extra inch in the waist. The collar of the shirt was a good fit, but Cal couldn't fill the jacket. The touch of the material on his skin disturbed him. This was a dead man's suit.

He looked at himself in the mirror. It would do. He began to knot the tie.

'How is it?' asked Mairi from the other side of the door.

'It's good. Come in. See what you think.'

She peered cautiously round the door, and then came into the room, looking him up and down, nodding her head in approval.

'Does it feel okay?'

'Fine.'

She stepped in front of him and began to adjust the tie. Cal watched her intently and felt his throat thicken, but she was oblivious to the effect she was having on him. Then she ran her hands down the front of the jacket to smooth it and stepped back, looking him up and down again.

'You look very handsome,' she smiled. 'Mary would be proud of you.'

With that, she turned, asking over her shoulder whether he wanted tea, and the moment was gone. As he followed her, Cal had to wonder whether there had ever been a moment.

Later, as they sat in the kitchen, Mairi noticed Cal adjusting the suit. 'Stop fussing. It looks as good as new. I think Colin only ever wore it the once himself.'

'D'you mind my asking, when did he die?'

'Two years ago.'

'It must have been hard for you.'

Mairi nodded. 'It wasn't much easier when he was alive, to be honest.'

Cal was taken aback.

'Colin liked his drink. I told you that already. It's not easy to live with that. It's not how I thought it would be.

I should have known better. He took a good drink before we married, but I thought he would stop.' She sniffed and smiled simultaneously. 'How often do you hear that? Why do women always think they can change their man?'

She sat forward, and played with a biscuit wrapper.

'He wasn't nasty with it, not physically anyway. He never laid a finger on me. But he could be vicious with his talk if he got in a mood. And he thought nothing of getting in the car to go drinking. And he'd justify it too. He used to say that it was easy to stop drink driving in the city, but how were country folk supposed to get to a hotel if they couldn't take their car? That was how he saw it. And it's what killed him of course. Coming back from town.' She shook her head.

'What happened,' asked Cal quietly after some moments.

'The car came off the road at a bend. They don't know if something was on the road or if he just lost control. They told me that at the speed he was going he had no chance. Such a waste.'

Colin Junior came through to the kitchen, now washed and smartly dressed. He immediately saw what Cal was wearing.

'That's my dad's suit,' he blurted.

'Yes,' said Mairi, 'Cal's just borrowing it for the funeral.'

'But it's dad's.'

'I know. It's just for the funeral,' she repeated.

'Look,' interjected Cal, 'if Colin's uncomfortable about it, I can wear something else.'

'No,' said Mairi sternly. 'You're just being silly Colin. Cal needs a suit for the funeral.'

'And he hasn't got one of his own?'

'Not with me, I'm afraid,' explained Cal.

Colin stomped out of the room.

'I'm sorry,' apologised Mairi.

'No need. It must be difficult for him.'

'He's very protective of his father.'

'You can understand that.'

'He's very like him too. It worries me. He's getting to that age and he's just being difficult. He wants to be like his dad. That's what all that hanging around the hotel is about.'

'That's just what kids do.'

'Maybe, but he's heard stories of what his dad was like and he wants to be the same. He needs male guidance in his life. All the people close to him are women.'

'He seems a good lad to me.'

'He is, and that's why I'm hopeful. When he drinks it's because he wants to be like his father, he drinks for show, to be one of the boys. His father drank for a reason.'

Mairi responded to the quizzical look on Cal's face.

'His father drank because he hated the fact he was adopted.'

18

'HE DIDN'T FIND out until he was at high school,' Mairi explained. 'And he found out, he wasn't told. His uncle blurted it out when he was drunk. It came as a shock. I suppose it was like you are feeling now. Everything he had thought about himself was wrong.'

'Did he ever find out who his real mother was?' asked Cal.

'No. He didn't want to. As far as he was concerned, she'd given him up and that was that. Maybe he'd have changed in time.'

'Did he know anything about her?'

'No. All he was told was that she'd been young and unmarried. He didn't ask any more.'

'And that's why he drank?'

'That's what I think.'

'I can understand. It's strange.'

'Don't start feeling like that until you know for sure.'

'But I do.'

'Okay,' said Mairi getting up and bringing the conversation to an end. 'I'll need to get ready.'

She was away for only a few minutes. Cal stiffened in surprise when she returned dressed elegantly in a black trouser-suit. Minimal make-up brought sophistication to her fresh face.

'That's a transformation,' he said admiringly. 'You look good.'

'Just the day for it,' she responded dismissively. 'We'd better get up to the house.'

'It's pouring.'

'It looks like it's on for the day,' observed Mairi, looking out the window.

'Will we take the car?'

'To Mary's?'

'We'll get wet by the time we get to the car anyway. No, get the umbrellas and we'll walk, for all the distance it is.'

If the wind had been of any strength they would have been soaked, but the rain poured straight down from the clouds and the umbrellas protected the four of them from all but splashes on their shoes. Cal shared a brolly with Mairi and the two of them huddled close as they made their way up the hill. Cal couldn't help enjoying being so close to her, but Mairi was distracted by the children, issuing rapid instructions about staying properly under their brolly.

Colin and Emma entered Mary's house cautiously, looking around as if they were expecting to see someone. Mairi began to lay the peats in the stove and Cal watched in admiration as the urbanely dressed figure skilfully tackled that most basic of tasks, setting a fire.

Then he noticed that Emma was crying. Mairi went straight to her and hugged her tightly.

'It's so empty and cold,' sobbed the girl.

'It's okay baby,' soothed her mother, caressing her hair and kissing her head. 'She's in a better place and she's not in pain any more.'

The girl buried her face in her mother's shoulder. Colin was determinedly not showing any emotion.

'She was like a granny to them. They were here so often.' Mairi's statement was uttered as an explanation to Cal, but had the dual purpose of putting into words what Emma herself wanted to say.

Colin left the room. Cal was uncertain about what to do. Eventually he used that reliable fall-back for moments of minor crisis and put the kettle on. Mairi smiled her approval.

'Can you check on Colin?' she requested.

The door to Mary's bedroom was open. Colin was sitting motionless on the edge of the bed.

'Are you okay?' Cal asked.

Colin jerked his head once.

'Your mum was wondering.'

'Is this where she died?' the boy asked curtly, looking at the bed.

Cal nodded. Colin breathed deeply. Cal sensed he wanted to say more.

'Were you with her?'

'Me and your mum.'

'What was it like?'

The forthright question took Cal aback and he struggled to answer.

'Peaceful,' he finally said and having got the first word out, the rest flowed easily enough. 'She was asleep and then she wasn't breathing any more. That's all. She wasn't in any pain. It's the way to go.' He cringed as he uttered the last sentence. 'I mean, she was in her own bed, she wasn't in a hospital ward or anything like that.'

'Or lying in a field.'

'What?'

'That's what happened to my dad. Bled to death on his own, lying in a field in the dark.'

'Jesus, Colin. How d'you know that? It might have been instant.'

'Nah. I know. I saw his death certificate. It was all these

medical terms, but I looked them up. He bled to death on his own with nobody near him to help.'

'Don't think like that. Even if you're right, chances are he wasn't conscious.'

'He was my dad and I know. I just do.'

'Well, don't think about it.'

'I'm not going to forget him.'

'That's not what I'm saying. Just don't think of that.'

'You're telling me this was a better way to die.'

'I'm not saying there is a good way to die. But the way it was for Mary, if there's a way to go, maybe that's the best.'

Cal was finding the conversation very difficult. He knew he was relying on clichés.

'I think you're talking crap,' Colin jibed. 'She shouldn't have died. Not yet. She should've had years left. She was killed by cancer and that's about as painful as it gets. And who were the loved ones? You and my mum?'

Cal was taken aback.

'My mum maybe, but who are you anyway? When was the last time you were here? I was here loads and I never saw you, not once.'

'What is all this?' asked Cal defensively.

'We were about the only family she had. And then when she dies, you appear from nowhere with your poser car, start taking over everything and now you're wearing my dad's clothes.'

Cal's anger flared. 'Listen, I know who I am and why I'm here. That woman was my mother and I'm not going to stand here and listen to some screwed up little mouth like you question me and what I do.'

'Your mother?' Colin repeated disbelievingly. 'You're making it up.'

Cal heard Mairi coming.

'Colin, don't do or say anything to upset your mother. Not today.'

'You're not my father and never will be,' Colin spat back.

Cal stalked out and met Mairi in the hallway.

'Is she okay?' he asked nodding towards the kitchen.

'She's lost her granny. That's how she sees it.'

Mairi's face crumpled. Cal placed his hands on her shoulder and pulled her gently towards him to comfort her. As he did so, Colin emerged from the bedroom and deliberately bumped against him as he walked passed. Their eyes met in a moment of mutual dislike.

Cal was in a ferment. His own words kept returning to him: 'my mother'. Finally, the tears welled up from deep inside and poured down his face and he sobbed sorely in Mairi's arms. They stood there, bound in sorrow, until they heard Emma announce that tea was ready. At the same instant, Cal's phone rang.

19

'HI. IT'S ME.' It was Lisa. 'I've got your birth certificate.'

'Hold on,' instructed Cal. 'It's the call I've been expecting,' he whispered apologetically to Mairi and began climbing the stairs to seek privacy. 'What does it say?'

'Nothing.'

'What d'you mean, nothing?' He was instantly deflated.

'Well, nothing unusual. It's got all the usual stuff you would expect to see, but nothing more.'

'Are you sure?' he persisted.

'I'll read it to you.'

She read quickly through all the details. His full name, when and where he was born, his father's name and occupation, his mother's maiden name, brief details of their marriage, the fact that his father had signed the certificate and the name of the registrar.

'And that's it, nothing more?'

'Nothing.'

'There must be.'

'There isn't, believe me. I...' Lisa stopped herself.

'What?' demanded Cal impatiently. 'What is it?'

'You never said what this was about,' she continued hesitantly, 'But I got an idea from what you said when you asked me to do this, or more from what you didn't say.'

'What about it?' Cal was confused.

'I asked the woman at the registry office if this showed that you were adopted.' Lisa paused to judge his reaction before going on. There was no sound from him. 'Well, she said that there's no chance. Your mum's name is on your full certificate, so that's who your mum is.'

'No, that can't be right,' exclaimed Cal in exasperation.

'I'm just telling you what she told me.'

'She said that, quite specifically told you that?'

'Yes. She said there could be no doubt.'

'I know that's wrong, I know it.' Cal's voice betrayed his disbelief and confusion. 'I've discovered things since I came here. I know I was adopted. The woman, my aunt who died. She was my mother. I know she was.'

'The woman said if you'd been adopted, there would be something on your birth certificate to say so. Details of a court order or something.'

'They must have worked it some way.' Cal was speaking aloud, but not to Lisa. He ended the call without any acknowledgement or thanks for what she'd done.

During the conversation he had been drawn into the room with the cache of letters. He pulled open the suitcase again, withdrew the boxes of letters and mementoes and emptied them onto the bed. The letters, the lock of hair, the identity bracelet, the clues that had set in train all the questions in his mind. He could look through them again and they would tell him the same story. Something was wrong, something didn't fit and he couldn't understand what it might be.

He heard Mairi's footsteps on the stairs. She entered, flushed from crying, but she was composed.

'Are you okay?' she asked. His face answered her question.

'What's wrong?'

'I don't understand,' he answered, picking up the letters and dropping them again beside him on the bed.

'What?'

'It's just not right. Something's wrong.' Cal was barely articulate.

'What is it? That call. Was it bad news?'

Cal held his head in his hands for a few moments and then sat up with a sigh.

'Not bad news, I don't suppose, but it's left me confused.'

'How?' Mairi sat down beside him.

'All that stuff I was talking about before we came here, about Mary having a baby. These letters, the identity bracelet.' He held it up for Mairi to see. 'I honestly thought that baby was me. I still do.'

'So what's changed?'

'My birth certificate. You said it would confirm it, but it doesn't. That's what the call was about. I can't figure it out.'

Mairi sat holding the plastic identity bracelet and remained silent.

'D'you think they might have kept the birth completely quiet and just registered me in my mum's name, just to keep Mary out of the picture altogether?' he continued.

'That would have been hard to do. It would have been hard to keep that secret,' she said softly.

'But people do. You hear about people having babies they didn't know they were expecting and babies being abandoned on doorsteps. It happens all the time.'

'That doesn't explain this,' said Mairi, holding up the identity tag. 'That came from a hospital. Just supposing Mary had the baby in secret and your mother went to the hospital claiming it as hers. They would have checked her over, they'd have known she was lying.'

'How else could they have done it without anyone knowing?'

'Maybe they didn't. Have you thought about that?'

'Mary had a baby, there's no question. This tag was her baby's.' He picked up the envelope and grasped the lock of hair from inside it and thrust it at Mairi. 'This was her baby's hair. Her best friend told me that she had a baby. I'm not wrong.'

'Yes, but maybe the baby wasn't you.'

Cal sat open mouthed, breathing deeply.

'That she had a baby isn't in doubt, Cal,' continued Mairi gently. 'The facts can't be denied with all this and what Kate-Anna told you. The evidence is there. What you don't have is evidence you were that baby. You made assumptions, you didn't have anything to back them up.'

'I did,' Cal argued stubbornly. 'She saw the baby grow up. Who else could that be? Mary was like a second mother to me all my life. Why would that be? My father resented me. Why would that be? She wanted to see me before she died. She kept all this stuff.'

'That only proves that she had a child, not that it was you. All the rest, it's just conjecture. The only fact you actually have about the identity of the baby is that it wasn't you. Your birth certificate tells you that. Why does it matter to you so much? You already had a mother you loved. Why do you so want to bury another one?'

They were interrupted by Colin shouting up from downstairs. 'That's it coming.'

Cal went over to the window and looked inland. Two sleek black vehicles were coming in the road. Even from half a mile away, he could clearly see the boxed shape and large windows of the hearse. Behind it came the sleek lines of the limousine.

'We'd better get downstairs,' said Mairi.

'I'll follow you in a minute,' answered Cal, his eyes fixed on the approaching cars.

Mairi came over to him and rested her hand on his shoulder.

'Cal, today will be hard enough. Don't make it worse for yourself.'

He put his hand to hers and grasped it for comfort, conscious of how delicate and soft it seemed in his grip. After a moment, she broke from him and went downstairs. He remained at the window as the cortege moved smoothly towards them. Only on the final stretch could he see through the glass to the flower-decked coffin. The long black cars were so fitting for their undertaking. Their classic looks, their gleaming black colour and their smooth motion so appropriate. In the end, after all is said and done, the only passages that mattered were the odysseys of birth and of death. The cars were the right chariots for the final journey.

The scene was at once, strangely, both personal and impersonal. In a sense Mary was home for the last time, but all he could see was a wooden box. Mary, dear Mary, was in there, but beyond him.

The hearse drove on past the house and out of sight again to find a suitable place to turn, a difficult manoeuvre on such a narrow road.

He went downstairs. Emma shyly offered him a cup of tea and Colin sat at the table drinking his, ignoring him with attitude. Cal carried his cup out of the back door.

The rain had passed for the moment, leaving a glistening landscape. The road, the metal fences, the grass and even the lochs looked refreshed in the weak sunlight. But more dark clouds were massing over the sea.

Clouds always seemed to be at the mercy of the wind, the small white puffs of a summer's day, the thin grey cover of a dull one, even the rolling mists. All propelled and shifted by the wind. Not these black clouds. They were their own masters, a threatening mass. To see that oncoming power in such an unbroken vista was intimidating indeed.

Approaching storms had scared Cal as boy. Even as a man, such natural forces made him conscious of his insignificance and helplessness.

The hearse reappeared and pulled to a halt outside the gate.

The perspective from Cal's position at the front of the house was that its sombre cargo was right beneath the oncoming cloud mass. And now it wasn't just his insignificance that troubled him, but his mortality too.

Could it be that he was no longer alone? If he was wrong about Mary, and his mind was slowly working its way to that conclusion, then there must be another of his blood. The question that he needed to answer now was, who?

20

CAL CRIED AGAIN when he saw Mary for the last time. The coffin was placed in an ante-room in the church and the lid removed for those who wished to say a final farewell. It is a comfort for the living to say that the dead are simply sleeping in everlasting repose, only their eyes closed and their heart stilled. Cal had learned the myth of this from the death of his parents, but it still unsettled him to see Mary now.

In her last hours the fullness of her face had been lost to the ravages of her illness. In death it had settled and flattened, her jawline subsiding into her neck. And she was so cold, cold like marble. Something vital was gone, the essence of what had made her who she was. The faithful believed it was the soul that had departed the shell of the body. Mary herself would have said so. Cal found himself inclined towards the more prosaic explanation that science provided. He had never been one to dwell on such fundamental questions. Until now.

Those who came to see her were believers. The confusing dichotomy was, what exactly were they paying tribute to?

If their belief was that these were the earthly remains of the woman they had known and the spirit had flown unto eternal salvation, why pay respect to the discarded husk?

Cal sat on a chair beside Mairi just inside the door of the room and watched as they filed through in ones and twos. Some touched her head or hand, others looked upon her in silence, a few muttered a prayer through their tears. As he watched Cal concluded that it was not a spiritual ritual, but an altogether more earthy want, the simple need to delay saying that last goodbye to a dear friend.

For Cal the final moment was a last look at a woman of good heart and hidden sorrow, a constant light in his life, now extinguished. Mairi became very upset and leaned over the corpse and kissed the forehead, the tears running down to the tip of her nose and quivering over the dead face as if it might drop in a desperate bid to restore life. The two of them embraced until Mairi's wave of sorrow receded.

The minister hovered in the corridor outside and when he heard Cal whisper words of comfort, he entered the room.

'Perhaps, if you're ready, we will start the service,' he suggested quietly.

Cal led Mairi by the hand into the main church hall.

He immediately saw that most people had not gone to see Mary's body. The front pews were filled and, although the numbers thinned towards the back of the church, there was not a bench that was empty. It was striking how many of the mourners were young. As they made their way down to the front of the church, Mairi nodded gestures of acknowledgement to familiar faces. The very front pew had been reserved for them as the closest relatives.

Mairi had been reluctant to take such a prominent position. 'I don't know that I should be there,' she had protested. But Cal had told her he needed her beside him. 'All these people will be wondering who I am.'

'They'll know who you are, don't worry about that.'

But she had been persuaded. Colin and Emma, whom Mairi had insisted should not see the remains, were already seated waiting for them.

As the coffin was carried to the front of the church by the undertakers, the only sound was their shoes creaking at every slow step. This could be the only time Mary had been walked down the aisle, Cal thought. Another pang of sadness brushed his heart.

The undertakers bowed in respect and retreated. It was so quiet that Cal felt as if he could hear the air move. It was disturbed only by the occasional sniff of restrained tears or a cough.

The coffin sat right in front of Cal on a wooden trestle. It was of traditional, solid dark oak with a tiered lid and brass handles. A wreath of red roses, carnations and orchids set among green foliage sat on top. That had been his sole contribution. The rest had been organised by Mary herself in anticipation of what was to come. The whole effect, from the church to the coffin was one of honest simplicity, with nothing ostentatious. It was in keeping with the woman herself.

After some minutes, a door opened and the chief elder and the minister emerged. The elder, dressed in a black three-piece suit, climbed the four steps into the pulpit and placed a large, leather-bound Bible on the pedestal, opening it at pages marked by a satin bookmark that bore the image of the burning bush.

The minister waited for him to leave the pulpit and then entered it himself. He seemed somehow different, to the man Cal had met only two nights before. Perhaps it was the black jacket and the grey trousers with black pin stripes, and the black vest with the stark white collar that gave him a more authoritarian appearance.

He looked down at the coffin before casting his eyes around the congregation. Then his hand dropped to his lapel and his thumb clicked on a microphone.

'Let us all sing to the Lord's praise in Psalm Forty,' he pronounced.

The words, written millennia before by a king in praise of the Almighty, rose in humble song as the precentor led the congregation, his every note seemingly with its own grace note. The congregation joined in after the first few words, their voices swelling to fill the void where musical instruments might be expected. Each individual voice had its own inflexion and flourish, but together they produced a soulful song that would be recognisable in the plains of Africa and the plantations of the American South. It was a root sound of humanity, the same now as ever it had been.

As the voices fell around him to staggered silence, Cal felt the goosebumps rise on his skin. It was easy, in the need to be cool and the dash to be stylish, to leave behind that which was truly lasting. His world only ever crossed that of his parents on ritual occasions like this, and always he was reminded why some traditions endured. He recognised how important the rites of death were for the living. Not for the dead. The viewing of the remains, the religious service and the formal burial were for those who lived on. Over and over these same ceremonies were repeated and all of it to bring comfort to the living.

After the singing, they stood in lengthy prayer. For the sermon, the minister took as his text John Chapter 6, verse 37 and talked of how those who came to Jesus would never be turned away. It was an uplifting message of hope and redemption.

There was no eulogising. The emphasis of the Presbyterian funeral service was on the message, not the person. Cal recalled how not so long before, even the name of the dead would not be mentioned and how cold and harsh that could be. It was a welcome comfort to hear Mary's name spoken with warm regard.

During the final psalm, the undertakers returned and lifted

the coffin onto their shoulders and carried it again to the back of the church. It was a solemn moment, the beginning of the very end. For those not going to the cemetery, and that included most of the older women, this was the valediction.

Cal and Mairi were the first to follow behind the minister, unconsciously pacing their steps in time with the singing. The wind gusted through the open door of the church bringing animation to the stillness within. The petals of the flowers on the coffin fluttered and the pages of the visitors' psalm books at the door rustled. For the moment, though, the clouds held their rain.

'This you'll need to do on your own,' said Mairi, leaving him standing just inside the door.

The congregation filed out slowly, each one shaking his hand. One or two gripped tightly and looked intently at him as they spoke their words of homage. He mumbled the same thanks to each of them.

The coffin was resting upon a bier. After everyone had left the church, a line formed behind it and when the undertaker saw that all was ready, he gave the signal for the hearse to move off. The men took turns in carrying the wooden beams that supported the coffin and in this way Mary MacCarl made her last journey through the village that she had known so well. Beyond the village boundary the coffin was loaded into the hearse and Cal took his place in the chief mourner's car for the few miles to the cemetery. Mairi was already waiting inside, as he had asked her to do. In times before, they would have had to sail on an open boat to the old cemetery.

The Atlantic sighed as the coffin was carried to the open grave, followed by the mourners, predominately male, but with some women among them. The older women, in keeping with tradition, chose not to be at the graveside.

The head undertaker distributed cards to those who had been designated as cord holders, each with the printed outline of a coffin and numbered positions marked around it. Typically, card holders would be family members, but Cal was the only family Mary had. Or at least, as he acknowledged silently, the only one who was known.

Finlay stood mournfully studying his card. He looked uncomfortable in his collar and black tie, his hair struggling with the wind. Gone was the bombast of their confrontation. He looked a lonely man.

The minister approached Cal and explained that Mary had requested the graveside prayer be in Gaelic. He then gathered everyone around the grave. The coffin sat over it on two wooden supports. Mary's mother tongue was an ancient language that some claimed had been spoken in the Garden of Eden. The sounds were familiar to Cal, and although their precise meaning was lost to him, the message was understandable enough, a plea for God's mercy on the soul now passing into eternity.

It was a bleak, sorrowful scene, although perhaps without wrenching sadness. There was an acceptance of the inevitable and thankfulness that Mary's passing freed her from pain.

The minister finished and then called on the card holders to take their positions. Cal stood at the head of the coffin and watched as another five figures came forward and were handed purple cords, which were tied to the brass handles of the coffin. To Cal's surprise, they included young Colin.

He didn't know the other three. One of them was of a similar age to Mary. He looked lost and forlorn in his grey Harris Tweed coat. Was he the one who had proposed to her in vain, all those years before? There was another older man wearing an ill-fitting suit with a jumper underneath, Finlay and a smartly-dressed man about his own age.

On the instruction of the head undertaker, the mourners gripped the cords and took the weight of the coffin. The supporting wooden slats were withdrawn and the coffin lowered slowly into its final resting place, scraping the sandy soil from the sides of the grave as it sank below the surface, away from the wind and the oncoming rain, the sounds of the ocean and the world of the living.

The men threw the cords onto the coffin and the minister prayed again. Then, at his gesture, Cal took a handful of soil from the heap at the graveside and cast it onto the coffin. He had done his duty by her.

Others followed, repeating the symbolic gesture. Finlay lingered longer than most. And Cal watched as Mairi too stood crying.

They departed slowly, despite the rain now weeping down, moving in small groups towards the gate of the cemetery.

Before the morning was gone, the grave would be filled in and Mary would be but a memory.

21

IN THE COMFORT of the car going back to the village, thoughts swept Cal's mind almost in time with the sweep of the rain outside. Reminisces of his aunt, of the things that made her unique in his memory. Consideration, too, of the mystery she had left behind. Mairi sat beside him, but little was said beyond her simple observation that, 'It's how she wanted it to be.'

The convoy swung into the car park of the hotel with a scrunch of tyres on stone. One woman, still wearing her hat from church, ran in to announce their arrival, although they could hardly have been missed. Everyone was wanting to do their bit.

Cal walked with Mairi into the hotel.

'Oh Calum,' said the woman who'd been stationed at the door, 'You get that coat off you. You must be soaked.'

He took no offence at being fussed over. It was part of what it had been like when he was at Mary's.

'It was a lovely service by the minister,' the woman continued. 'She would have enjoyed it herself.'

'Yes, I think you're right,' he answered softly, smiling at the unconscious humour of the comment.

'Well, come away in. The girls have got the food ready.'

A number of tables were lined together along one wall of the small dining room, draped with white linen cloths, which gave the effect of one long table. Ranged across it were plates of food, far too much food. Cal was glad to see that some of the sandwiches were made of the thick-sliced, black-crusted bread baked on the island. Otherwise, the sausage rolls, quiche and Chinese chicken were indistinguishable from the fare at so many buffet meals. He noticed there was soup too, broth. The bread and the broth would do him fine.

He joined the line filing past the food and then made his way to the table. Mairi took a place beside him, the minister sat on the other side.

After saying grace they ate. The sombre silence was gone as people chatted, and even laughed at some recalled incident.

'So what are your plans now, Calum?' asked the minister conversationally.

The question made Cal think. On his journey north the plan had been very simple, to sell the house and take the money. So much had changed these past few days and the thought of the money had barely entered his mind. He had become consumed by Mary's past and his own.

'I need to go back to the city first of all. Then I'll have time to think things through.'

'It must have come as a shock, as it did to us all.'

'I'd no idea. She never said.'

'I suppose she thought there was nothing you could do, so why upset you?'

The minister's open face and sympathetic manner encouraged Cal to talk.

'Perhaps, but there are things I would've like to have known. Questions I wanted to ask.'

'Lucky are the ones who can pass to the Lord leaving

nothing unanswered behind them. There are always questions, but only of detail. She knew you loved her and when all is said and done, that's what's important.'

A person sitting on the other side drew the minister's attention away.

'He's right,' said Mairi.

'I suppose so,' accepted Cal. 'But I think she wanted me to know. That's why she had you call me. She wanted to tell me and it needed to be done face to face. But it was too late.'

A figure approached from across the room, casting a shadow as he reached them. It was Finlay. Even when he tried to speak quietly, his voice was loud. Cal's gaze was drawn by the red weal forming where the buttoned shirt collar was rubbing Finlay's neck.

'I know now is not the time,' he began, 'but before you go I want you to remember what I said.'

'Oh, Finlay!' admonished Mairi.

'You're right, it's not the time,' said Cal emboldened by Mairi's presence. 'I wasn't likely to forget what you said and I won't. Nothing's decided. It won't be for a while.'

Finlay glared at him and then strode to the door, collected his coat and went out into the rain.

'What is it with that man?'

'He's lacking in social graces, I know,' said Mairi in a placatory tone. 'He doesn't know how to deal with people. He just wanted to speak to you because he doesn't know if he'll see you again. He'll be walking in that road now and glad to be away from all of this. He's so used to his own company that he prefers it that way, but he's lonely at the same time.'

'You're always defensive of him.'

'I don't think there's anything bad about Finlay, it's just that the world has passed him by. Mary wouldn't hear a word against him. *She* was his real protector.'

Finlay's departure was a prompt to others to leave. They

had come to honour the passing of one of their own and they had done so. Much of the food remained. It was always the way.

Mairi suggested that he should leave his place at the table and make himself available for people to say goodbye. One woman came towards him. It had been warm enough for her to take off her coat, but her hat remained a fixture on her head.

'Well, the two of you look very handsome together,' she smiled.

'Oh, Mabel,' Mairi rebuked her.

In mock conspiracy, Mabel took Cal by the arm and turned him away from Mairi, but spoke loudly enough for her to hear.

'She's a good woman and she needs a man. She's been long enough on her own. You like her, I can tell.'

Cal laughed with embarrassment, but couldn't think of a riposte. He was acutely conscious that his face was bright red.

Mabel released him and turned to Mairi.

'A handsome man like that. You shouldn't let him go.'

'Oh Mabel, eesht!'

They continued the gentle banter and Cal saw how tactile they were, touching each other's arms before Mabel bustled off to get her coat.

'She's full of mischief, that one,' chuckled Mairi, but he could sense an undertow of embarrassment.

'Mum, can we go?'

It was Colin, who had overheard the whole interchange and was evidently displeased.

'Do you have to? Now?' asked Cal.

'I'll need to get them home. It's been a long morning.'

'Who did they travel with?'

'Roddy. They went with Roddy.' She continued when she saw the inquisitive look on his face. 'He's from the village. He was next to Colin with the cord at the graveside.'

'What was his connection with Mary?'

'She was close friends with his family,' she shrugged. 'He's a nice man, Roddy. He takes Colin fishing and sometimes helps me with work in the house.'

'Finlay'll love that.'

She smiled shyly.

'Why don't you come back with us?'

'No. It's okay.'

'When are you leaving?'

'Tomorrow most likely.'

'Will you be back?'

'I don't know. There's the house to be emptied. Maybe I can find out more if I do it. I'll call you.'

'So this won't be the last time we see you?'

'You won't get rid of me that easily.'

Mairi looked to the floor and then stepped towards him and hugged him.

'It was good of you to come. She knew. She knew you were there.' Mairi was crying.

Cal put his arms around her waist.

'Isn't it me who's supposed to thank people for coming?'

She looked at him, her eyes moist.

'Thank you for calling me and for looking after her,' Cal said sincerely. 'For everything. Thank you.'

When they released each other, he saw Emma and Colin behind her, the youth staring hard at him. Another figure, Roddy, was waiting for them at the door. Colin went ahead and began talking to him. It was clear to Cal how comfortable they were with each other.

The room was empty now except for the waitresses clearing up. Mairi and her children left with Roddy. She paused and turned to wave, trying to hold back the tears. Cal stood in the middle of the room and watched her go. Alone again.

22

AS CAL PULLED off his shoes in his hotel room, he realised he was still wearing the suit he had borrowed. It lifted him to think there would be a reason to see Mairi again before he left, although he sensed he would gain little from it. It was apparent that his attraction to her was not reciprocated, although he clearly inspired some affection or emotion in her. Her tearful goodbye told him that.

He had to acknowledge that his feelings for her were different from the usual predatory mode. It was something about simply being with her, sensing her near to him that excited him. It was much more than the animal impulse of assessing a willing sex mate. It wasn't love, not yet, although it might become so. He could only guess at that because he had never been in love. He had felt this about two other women before, but those relationships had never developed because he feared the limitations they would impose. He had reassured himself that he hadn't been ready, unsettled that his emotions had taken him so close. This time, though, he felt more comfortable. It was unforced, natural. But there was nothing coming back. Nothing that was the same, anyway. The suit was still damp and he folded it over a chair beside the radiator. Removing the shirt was a relief and he lay on the bed in his shorts.

The minister had asked him what his plans were. He could easily make the evening ferry, but that was not what he wanted to do. He didn't want to dash away with things unsaid and loose ends left untied. And he had to collect his car from Mary's house. Her letters were still scattered on the bed in the upstairs room.

There was no rush. His body relaxed and he drifted off to sleep.

The sun had followed the storm clouds and it was bright outside when he woke. The light and his refreshed mind brought clarity of thought. Mary was not his mother, he knew that now. Mairi had made sense when she said it was the only fact which had evidence to support it. He had not been adopted. His parents were truly his mother and father.

It perturbed him how ready he had been to accept that they might not be. That hadn't hurt as much as it should. He should have had more resistance to the idea. His mother, so proud of him and so dear. Even as she struggled painfully in a fight she knew she would lose, her eyes would light up when she saw him and she would speak only of what mattered to him and his future. She had given everything for him and yet he had questioned her place so readily. His betrayal hurt now. It really hurt. And his father. Despite the tensions between them, the fact was that his father had always been there and had been willing to sacrifice his own dreams for his boy. Maybe he resented it at times, but he had done it and his son had not been grateful. He would be now.

Cal resigned himself to thinking that he would never know who Mary's child had been. A child she had given birth to and then given away, keeping only a few precious memories. If it had been only that, then he could have accepted the child would always be unknown to him.

What if the child had been raised on the island? Snippets of information and snatches of conversation slipped in and out of his mind like objects picked over by torchlight in a darkened room. They began to connect, forming fuller pictures that asked more questions. Why had Roddy been one of the cord-holders? Why was his connection to Mary deemed any more than that of other men of the village, who would had known her for a lot longer?

And what of Finlay? A difficult, isolated man, whose grief had been so intense. Mary had chosen him to be among the few who lowered her to her final rest. And Mairi had said he knew the house better than she did. He worked Mary's croft for her. And there was the way he wanted the house for his own. Cal had connected that with Mairi, but perhaps it had not been that at all.

And then there was Mairi's late husband, an orphan who had moved across the island to a village with which he had no connection.

Cal tried to keep his imagination in check. It had already guided him to conclusions that had been embarrassingly wrong. He must focus on his own future. The past was just that.

On that thought, he ordered a taxi from reception, freshened up and put on his own clothes and then sat by the window, waiting.

From his city apartment he could look right into people's lives in the buildings opposite. Below were the streets and cars, the windows and lights of the domestic and commercial packed together. There was always something happening, something to see, the bustle of the city. He could set his watch by looking outside. The early rush, the mid-morning lull, the build-up through the afternoon to the mad scramble of evening. He could even take a good guess at what day of the week it was from the hustle below.

This view was altogether different. The mutating light, the movement of the water of the loch, the birds and wildlife oblivious to his presence. Constantly changing and yet somehow timeless.

Cal drifted in thought until the ringing of the room phone made him jump. His taxi had arrived. He draped the suit over his arm and went downstairs.

The driver had expected a fare to town and sped along the roads, anxious not to miss a more lucrative fare. Cal was at Mairi's house within five minutes. Her car wasn't there and he wondered if the journey had been wasted. There was every chance that the place would be unlocked, in the island way and he would be able to leave the suit inside. But without her being there, the journey was still worthless.

He saw no sign of activity, but knocked on the side door to make sure he didn't surprise anyone. Not expecting a reply, he turned the handle and the door opened. He placed the suit over the back of a chair. As he turned to go, he thought he should leave a note and looked around for a scrap of paper, but nothing caught his eye. As he considered what to do, the inside door opened abruptly and young Colin stood looking at him.

'What are you doing here?' he demanded belligerently.

'The suit. I was bringing it back.' Cal gestured to the chair.

'The suit. My dad's suit.'

'Your dad's suit.'

'So you've done it.'

'Is your mum in?'

'No.'

There was no more information forthcoming.

'Well, d'you know where she might be?'

'Nuh.'

'Could I maybe write her a note?'

'Tell me. I'll tell her.' Colin's tone was still sharp.

'Colin, what's making you so angry with me?'

'Nothing.'

'You spoke clearly enough this morning.'

'So you know.'

'Not really. You're angry that Mary died and that your dad died. I know that. What I don't get is why that's my fault.'

'I didn't say it was.'

'Well, it seems like it.'

'I told you. I don't like people trying take my dad's place.'

'Come on,' protested Cal. 'How d'you figure that?'

'His suit. Trying to show off to me with your car. My mum. You're never away from her. And then you claim your Mary's son.'

Cal rubbed his forehead with his hand.

'That was a mistake,' he said sheepishly.

'Some mistake.'

'Your mum'll explain. If you're interested.'

'I'm not.'

'Alright Colin, you think you're a straight talker. Let's see if you can take it as well as give it out. I don't want to replace your dad. I never knew the man. Your mum? She's been great. Without her I wouldn't really have known what to do. And yeah, your mum's a good looking woman. But that's it. No Colin, there's only one guy in here trying to replace your dad, and that's you. Don't try and be him or what you think he was.' Emma appeared behind her brother and Cal could see the concern in her face. 'I've said enough and you'll not listen anyway. There's your dad's suit. Don't worry, I'll not be back.'

He strode out of the house. Despite his anger, there was something to be admired in the way the boy had stood up for his father against another adult. Most kids his age would have been reduced to impotent silence. Would he, Cal, have been the same? He doubted it.

He and Colin had hit it off that first night and it was a

pity that it had gone sour. That had all come from the boy seeing Cal in his father's suit. And was he so wrong? Cal had no interest in being a father to someone else's children, but he did have an interest in their mother. It was only natural Colin would resent it.

He re-ran the conversation in his head as he went up the brae to Mary's house. There was really no way back. Why should he care anyway, when would he ever see him again?

The house had a despondent air. The long grass was bowed and lifeless, beaten down by the earlier rain and the wind shifted without vigour. Cal walked round the path to the door, the conversation with Colin still in his mind. Something the boy had said niggled him and he was trying to remember what it was. Then as he pushed the side door open, it came to him. Suddenly, Cal knew.

23

THERE WAS STILL a little warmth in the kitchen from the fire that Mairi had lit that morning. Not much, but enough to keep away any chill. Cal packed more peats into the stove. He was getting more adept at it now.

Everything made sense and fitted together. He had decided earlier in the hotel that he would let it all go and live for tomorrow, but now he needed to speak to Mairi one more time. If he remained here, he would see her coming home and could intercept her. She must know. She would have to tell him. Her house was out of sight from the kitchen, but he could see it and every car coming in the road from upstairs.

He bounded up to the bedroom where he had left the letters scattered on the bed, gathered them up carefully and put them back in the box along with the identity tag and lock of hair, then returned it to the top of the wardrobe. He no longer had a claim to them.

An hour later there was still no sign of Mairi's return. His limbs were getting stiff from sitting by the window and he got up to get the blood flowing again. He went round the house making sure everything was in order. It was an upsetting experience. It was the little things that hit him. The women's magazine in the rack by the television, the packet of biscuits in the cupboard, the mail that had arrived that day, that would never be answered. Mary was gone now and in time the only physical mark left would be her gravestone at the cemetery. That was the one place he wanted to see again before he left. It seemed pointless to keep waiting for Mairi. He would see her at her place and if that meant speaking to her in Colin's presence, then that's what he'd have to do.

The breeze had picked up and the storm clouds were gone. The sun was falling to the western horizon. The end of another day. People were returning to their domestic condition – be it happy, sad, loving, longing, content, frustrated. And tomorrow they would rise to another day of the same. But here in this place, at this house, the sun was going down on the end of era. Nothing here would ever be the same again.

Another family might establish themselves and the place may come alive again, but it would be different for those who had known what had been before. And when time took them away, then nobody would remember. All around him on this ancient land, civilisations and generations had lived and died and the lives they had led, the customs and ties that had bound them, were lost and unknown.

There were enough physical clues for the archaeologists to understand how they might have lived. They could piece together a picture of how they provided for themselves, something of their rituals; there was evidence of their deaths. But no one could ever really know their lives, who they were, their loves and sorrows.

The records could not explain why a mother had killed her baby, only that she had. One could guess at the character of the young man who fled across the ocean to evade the law and married the daughter of a Native American tribal chief. One could guess, but could never really know, and nobody who did know was left to tell. The war memorial listed the names of the dead from foreign fields, but not of the blighted lives of the mothers and the sweethearts who were left.

Further back there were no records, except perhaps tales that had become legends to tell of the endurance of the young man who returned to his girl, of the mothers raising families alone when their man did not come back from the fishing, the disruption of the families forced out of their homes, the heroism of the farmer dying before marauding hordes to protect all that was his.

The records would show that this day Mary MacCarl had been buried, but tell nothing of who and what she was.

Cal was now driving away from the house, moved to seek a view of where she lay for perhaps the last time. Driving east with the sun behind him, the road and moor were cast in a palette of soft tones. The road was empty. He was chased by the mad dog again as he roared by, then his route took him round to the west. Before him hung the sun, golden above the sea. Cal tried to keep his eyes on the road, but they were constantly drawn to the beauty before him. It was only when the way dipped towards the shore and the sea was hidden that his full attention returned to the road ahead. There was another car parked beside the cemetery. It was Mairi's.

Cal had not expected to find her here, but then why wouldn't she be?

He walked through the cemetery and saw her at Mary's grave, crouched next to it with her back to him. It looked as though she was examining the cards on the bouquets that had been laid on top of the mound.

'Mairi,' he called, but his voice was thrown away by the sea breeze. The cellophane around the flowers crackled.

'Mairi!' he shouted more loudly, but again she didn't hear. It wasn't until he was almost level with her that he saw she was actually tending to the grave next to Mary's. She turned round, startled.

'Oh Cal! You gave me a fright.'

'I was calling, but you couldn't hear me. I'm sorry.'

'Oh Mairi,' he murmured, opening her arms to console her.

He glanced at the stone on the grave she had been tending. The inscription surprised him and his neck muscles flexed involuntarily as he tried to stop himself doing a double take. The name said 'Colin Nicolson' and the dates fitted.

'Your name's Nicolson isn't it?'

Her head nodded once against him.

They stood for a time in mutual consolation, the wind buffeting them and the ocean falling onto the sand below. Then, Mairi pulled away, searching in her pocket for a handkerchief. Cal placed his hands on her shoulders and stared into her eyes.

'I know Mairi. I really do know now. And you do too.' He knew he was right. 'I didn't even try to find out. I'd let it drop and then it came to me. It's been staring at me the whole time. Colin, your Colin, was Mary's baby.' He watched her hair dancing about her bowed head. 'You tried to make it so obvious to me and I was so caught up in my own ideas that I didn't see it. He was adopted, he chose to stay over beside her and they were close. But it wasn't until young Colin said to me today that I'd taken his dad's place at the funeral that it clicked. And now I see that she's buried beside him. I'm sorry. I've been a fool, and I've made it worse for you.'

Mairi took his hand in hers and began to walk him towards the perimeter of the graveyard.

'I didn't know Nicolson was your name,' he went on. 'Otherwise I might have noticed it before. I didn't even see it today at the funeral. I never asked.'

At the fence they looked out to the Atlantic. The water frothed and fizzed up the shore and then slipped back, smoothing the sand. They stood together watching the sun touch the horizon. Cal gave her space to speak, but she wasn't ready yet. And he was in no hurry. With the wind pulling the hair off her face and the golden light lifting her dark eyes and colouring her skin, he couldn't take his eyes off her.

Eventually he asked, 'Why couldn't you just tell me?'

'It was difficult,' she said, biting her lip.

Fearing that she might cry again, Cal tried for levity.

'So that makes Colin what? My cousin? So you're my cousin-in-law. Your boy is going to love that. Related to me. I know he's a Nicolson, but strictly speaking he's a MacCarl. And that's what she used to say to me all the time. 'The last of the line,' she'd say. Well it's good to know I'm not, not really.'

'You are, Cal.'

'I know his name is Nicolson, but his dad was really a MacCarl.'

'No, he wasn't.'

'Alright, I suppose strictly speaking he'd carry the name of the Canadian guy, but he wouldn't want to have the name of a family that didn't want him. No, he was a MacCarl.'

'No Cal, he wasn't.' Mairi turned to look at him. 'I was.'

24

ON THE EDGE of the bay a roller crashed loudly against the cliffs and a plume of spray arced through the air and seawater poured off the rock. A corresponding explosion rocked Cal inside. Mairi's revelation collided with everything he was sure of. It was as if he had been dealt a physical blow.

His eyes reconnected with hers. The physical motions were faster than the processes of his brain.

'*I* was Mary's baby,' she repeated, taking his hand again. The intensity of her stare was too much for him and he looked to the sea again.

'You?'

'Yes, me. Mary was my mother.'

The shock was too much. He pulled his hand from her's in hurt bewilderment. He couldn't speak and he couldn't walk away.

'Cal.'

A lesser wave thudded onto the rock. Miniscule spits of water splashed onto their faces. Mairi waited for him to respond. It took some time.

'You didn't say?' His voice strained and angry.

'I...' she began, but Cal didn't let her continue.

'You made a fool of me.'

'Cal, please. I didn't know until the night before she died. As she lay dying... that's when she told me. It's a shock to me too.'

Her plea mollified him. 'Is this what she was going to tell me?'

'She wanted you to hear it from her. But she deteriorated too quickly.'

'She had a lifetime to tell me. And you. Why leave it until the end?'

'Maybe there was never a right time before.'

'Tell me what she said.'

'Not here. Let's go down to the shore.'

They climbed the fence and jumped down the rocks onto the dry, soft sand, then made for the firmer, wet sand and walked slowly across the bay leaving a clear trail of imprints, the only marks on the empty shore. The sun had slipped farther down the sky and was sinking below the horizon, the waves flickering against its orange canvas.

'She knew the end was near. We were talking and it got quite intense, the things that are always left unsaid. I'd always known I was adopted, my parents never hid that from me. They were good people and I was happy and didn't give it much thought until I had Colin. Just having him there, holding my own baby, made me think how anyone could give away their child. I said that to her. When I think of it now, it must have been a knife to her heart.'

Cal nodded, watching the sand beneath their feet.

'That's when she told me. She wanted me to understand.' Mairi caught a cry as it built up within her.

'How was she?'

'It just all came out from her. All the years of keeping her emotions in check just came away. She was so distraught I thought she was going to die there and then.'

The grains of sand that had been so clear to Cal moments

before, now blurred. Mairi came close to him and wrapped her arms around him.

'You worked out the story. It's just as you said. She'd been in Canada and she fell for a man who didn't stand by her. She forgave him in the end. To herself. He was dead. Things were different then and he was young. They both were. I think she still loved him, I really do. I think that's why she never married, although she didn't say. It still hurt her after all these years. I was born in Glasgow. She was vague about how my parents got me, but it wasn't chance that they were from up here. She said it had been 'arranged' by a friendly nurse, but she didn't go into specifics and there was so much I wanted to hear I didn't ask. You guessed it all, except that you thought it was a boy she had.'

'Who else knows?'

'Just you and me. Your father and grandparents knew, but not that it was me. I don't even think my own parents knew who she was. The nurse was a friend of theirs, but all they ever knew was that the mother was unmarried. They never met. She said she'd sat with me after I was born, just like I had with Colin, and that it was so unbearable I had to be taken away quickly.'

'But she knew you were here?'

'Only that I was with an island family. The nurse had promised her that. But she didn't know where. She says she saw me as a wee girl in town with my mother and knew immediately I was hers. Said she used to watch me playing in the park. Imagine that, your own child and not able to even speak to her.'

'If you didn't know, why did you move across the island to the house across the road from her?'

'Chance. What I told you was true. Colin liked it over this side, the fishing and everything, and the house was cheap. The only thing that I didn't say was that Colin and I got together because we knew we were both adopted and we connected on that.'

'And the graves side by side?'

'I only found that out this morning. That's what I was thinking about when you came. She arranged the funeral herself and she must have arranged the plot too. She'd have known that's where I would go when my time came, next to Colin. And she wanted to be near me.'

Mairi's composure collapsed and she sobbed pitifully. Cal held her to him as the sun slipped below the skyline. The man of only days before might have had seduction on his mind, believing that at this time, in this light, in this beautiful, isolated place, any woman would be for the taking. But everything was different now and he held her sobbing heart close to him and did his best to soothe her sorrow.

Later, when Mairi was calmer, they sat on a rock mass and watched the water roll up the shore.

'How do you feel?' she asked.

'Sad. How could I be anything but? At least she had the chance to tell you. You held each other like a mother and daughter should. And that's more important than me being told. She was content, Mairi. When she went, she was ready. You could tell.'

'We were pals right from when we came here and she called in to say hello. It's only looking back on it that I can see she was like a mother to me, only I didn't know what was behind it.'

'Why didn't she say?'

'I don't know. She might have been afraid of losing me twice. Or maybe if I'd said I was looking for my birth mother, she'd have told me.'

Darkness was swallowing the dusk and they retraced their steps back into the cemetery.

'Are you okay?' asked Mairi, breaking the silence of thought that had descended.

'It's a lot to take in.'

'I know.'

'Are you going to tell people?'

'I don't think I will.'

'Secrets again? Look where it got us.'

'What's to be gained? Mary never told them, so that's how she must have wanted it. I'm not going to try to change it.'

'You'll tell the kids though?'

'Someday. They're too raw just now.'

'Then how are you going to explain the house?'

'The house?'

'It's yours now. I've no claim on it.'

'No!' Mairi protested. 'That's not right. It should be yours.'

'When I came here that was what was on my mind. I'm ashamed to admit it, but it was. Not now. And anyway, I don't deserve it.'

'What do you mean?'

'Listen, Mary was a big part of my life and these last few years I ignored her, or as good as. And when I came here, I looked at that house in terms of the money I could get for it. Well, that's not right. My family – our family – has ties here and I don't trust myself not to throw that away.'

Cal glanced at Mairi and saw again how attractive she was. He had developed an attraction to her which now seemed inappropriate. He would have to look upon her differently now and that would not be easy.

'So what next?' she asked.

'I go home.'

He thought of Lisa and the shoddy way he had treated her. To remedy that would be a priority. After that, he didn't know. Wait for the next big chance, probably. But he would do so understanding that it couldn't be the sole purpose of his life.

'And what about you? Might Roddy be playing a part in your future?'

She blushed. 'Maybe. We'll see.'

They came level with the grave again. Cal crouched down, touched his fingers to his lips, kissed them and placed them lightly on the fresh earth, then they walked on.

Some other books published by **LUATH** PRESS

The Road Dance
John MacKay
ISBN 1 84282 040 0
PBK £6.99

Why would a young woman, dreaming of a new life in America, sacrifice all and commit an act so terrible that she severs all hope of happiness again?

Life in the Scottish Hebrides can be harsh – 'The Edge of the World' some call it. For the beautiful Kirsty MacLeod, her love of Murdo and their dream of America promise an escape from the scrape of the land, the repression of the church and the inevitability of the path their lives would take. But the Great War looms and Murdo is conscripted. The village holds a grand Road Dance to send their young men off to battle. As the dancers swirl and sup, the wheels of tragedy are set in motion.

With a gripping plot that subtly twists and turns, vivid characterisation and a real sense of time and tradition, this is an absorbing, powerful first novel. The impression it made on me will remain for some time.
THE SCOTS MAGAZINE

Heartland
John MacKay
ISBN 1 905222 11 4
PBK £6.99

A man tries to build for his future by reconnecting with his past, leaving behind the ruins of the life he has lived. Iain Martin hopes that by returning to his Hebridean roots and embarking on a quest to reconstruct the ancient family home, he might find new purpose.

But as Iain begins working on the old blackhouse, he uncovers a secret from the past which forces him to question everything he ever thought to be true.

Who can he turn to without betraying those to whom he is closest? His ailing mother, his childhood friend and his former love are both the building and stumbling blocks to his new life.

Where do you seek sanctuary when home has changed and will never be the same again?

It is so refreshing to read a novel which is neither 'chick-lit', nor about abused childhoods or city chic... a gripping plot full of credible characters.
THE SCOTS MAGAZINE

Lewis and Harris: History and Pre-History
Francis Thompson
ISBN 0 946487 77 4
PBK £5.99

The fierce Norsemen, intrepid missionaries and mighty Scottish clans – all have left a visible mark on the landscape of Lewis and Harris. This comprehensive guide explores sites of interest in the Western Isles, from pre-history through to the present day.

Harsh conditions failed to deter invaders from besieging these islands or intrepid travellers from settling, and their legacy has stood the test of time in an array of captivating archaeological remains from the stunningly-preserved Carloway Broch, to a number of haunting standing stones, tombs and cairns. With captivating tales passed down through generations, Francis Thompson introduces us to his homeland and gives us an insight into its forgotten ways of life.

Scottish Roots
Alwyn James
ISBN 1 84282 090 7
PBK £6.99

For anyone interested in researching their family history, *Scottish Roots* provides an excellent, comprehensible step-by-step guide to tracing your Scottish ancestry. Using the example of two Scots trying to discover their roots, Alwyn James illustrates how easy it is to commence the research process and gradually compile a worthwhile family tree. He navigates the reader through the first steps of sourcing family details, making contact with distant relatives and preparing to collate any new information.

Now in its twentieth year of publication, this new and updated edition includes information on how to access family data utilising electronic resources and the Internet – a must if conducting research from an overseas base. A very welcome addition to the family library.

Luath Press Limited

committed to publishing well written books worth reading

LUATH PRESS takes its name from Robert Burns, whose little collie Luath (*Gael.*, swift or nimble) tripped up Jean Armour at a wedding and gave him the chance to speak to the woman who was to be his wife and the abiding love of his life. Burns called one of 'The Twa Dogs' Luath after Cuchullin's hunting dog in Ossian's *Fingal*. Luath Press was established in 1981 in the heart of Burns country, and is now based a few steps up the road from Burns' first lodgings on Edinburgh's Royal Mile. Luath offers you distinctive writing with a hint of unexpected pleasures. Most bookshops in the UK, the US, Canada, Australia, New Zealand and parts of Europe, either carry our books in stock or can order them for you. To order direct from us, please send a £sterling cheque, postal order, international money order or your credit card details (number, address of cardholder and expiry date) to us at the address below. Please add post and packing as follows: UK – £1.00 per delivery address; overseas surface mail – £2.50 per delivery address; overseas airmail – £3.50 for the first book to each delivery address, plus £1.00 for each additional book by airmail to the same address. If your order is a gift, we will happily enclose your card or message at no extra charge.

ILLUSTRATION: IAN KELLAS

Luath Press Limited
543/2 Castlehill
The Royal Mile
Edinburgh
EH1 2ND
Scotland
Telephone: 0131 225 4326 (24 hours)
Fax: 0131 225 4324
Email: sales@luath.co.uk
Website: www.luath.co.uk